D0343125

The
Mother-
Daughter
Book
Club

The Mother-Daughter Book Club

Heather Vogel Frederick

Aladdin Paperbacks
New York London Toronto Sydney

If you purchased this book without a cover, you should be aware that this book is stolen property. It was reported as "unsold and destroyed" to the publisher, and neither the author nor the publisher has received any payment for this "stripped book."

This book is a work of fiction. Any references to historical events, real people, or real locales are used fictitiously. Other names, characters, places, and incidents are the product of the author's imagination, and any resemblance to actual events or locales or persons, living or dead, is entirely coincidental.

ALADDIN PAPERBACKS
An imprint of Simon & Schuster Children's Publishing Division
1230 Avenue of the Americas, New York, NY 10020
Copyright © 2007 by Heather Vogel Frederick
All rights reserved, including the right of reproduction in whole or in part in any form.
ALADDIN PAPERBACKS and related logo are registered trademarks of Simon & Schuster, Inc.
Also available in a Simon & Schuster Books For Young Readers hardcover edition.
Designed by Lucy Ruth Cummins
The text of this book was set in Chaparral.
Manufactured in the United States of America
First Aladdin Paperbacks edition April 2008
2 4 6 8 10 9 7 5 3
The Library of Congress has cataloged the hardcover edition as follows:
The Mother-Daughter Book Club / Heather Vogel Frederick.—1st ed.
p. cm.
Summary: When the mothers of four sixth-grade girls with very different personalities pressure them into forming a book club, they find, as they read and discuss *Little Women*, that they have much more in common than they could have imagined.
[1.Interpersonal relations—Fiction. 2.Books and reading—Fiction. 3. Mothers and daughters—Fiction. 4. Clubs—Fiction. 5. Alcott, Louisa May, 1832–1888—Fiction. 6.Concord (Mass.)—Fiction.]
I. Title.
PZ7.F87217Mot 2007
[Fic]—dc22
2006024818
ISBN-13: 978-0-689-86412-4 (hc.)
ISBN-10: 0-689-86412-4 (hc.)
ISBN-13: 978-1-4169-7079-8 (pbk.)
ISBN-10: 1-4169-7079-7 (pbk.)

For Marjorie Hamlin—children's librarian, teacher, mentor, and friend—whose "book club" many springtimes ago helped launch a fledgling writer

The Mother-Daughter Book Club

AUTUMN

"Once upon a time, there were four girls, who had enough to eat and drink and wear, a good many comforts and pleasures, kind friends and parents, who loved them dearly, and yet they were not contented."

—Louisa May Alcott, *Little Women*

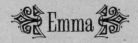

Emma

"'It's so dreadful to be poor!' sighed Meg, looking down at her old dress."

"Nice skirt, Emma," calls Becca Chadwick, giving me the once-over as I head down the aisle of the school bus looking for a seat.

This is not a compliment and I know it and she knows it. Blushing, I slide into the first empty spot I find. My brother Darcy passes me, heading for the last few rows, which, by tradition, are reserved for eighth graders.

Behind me, I hear Becca whisper something to Ashley Sanborn. I hunch down and smooth a crease in my skirt, my stomach clenching in all-too-familiar anxiety. It's starting already. I'd hoped maybe sixth grade would be different.

"Must have been a big back-to-school sale at the thrift store," says Ashley, her lame attempt at sarcasm producing a burst of laughter from Becca.

As the bus doors whoosh shut and we lurch forward down Lowell Road, I force myself to ignore them both and look out the window instead. The familiar scenery is soothing, and I feel myself relax a little as we cross the quiet waters of the Concord River and pass stately old colonial houses and meadows hemmed by time-worn stone walls. In a few weeks the leaves on all the trees will start to turn, quilting the woods with New England's famous blaze of yellow and scarlet and orange.

Here and there amongst the thickets I spot fat clusters of wild Concord grapes. They'll be ripe soon, and just thinking about the way the thick purple skins burst when I bite down, releasing the sour juiciness inside, makes my mouth start to water.

As we turn onto Barnes Hill Road and begin our slow circle back toward town, I pull a notebook from my backpack and open to a fresh page. "Ode to September," I write across the top. I chew the eraser on my pencil, pondering my opening line. But instead of writing verse, I find myself stewing about how much I hate the first day of school.

I never used to. When I was little, I could hardly wait for it to start. I'd get all excited about my new lunchbox and pencils and stuff, and I'd wear my new shoes around for weeks to break them in.

Then a couple of years ago, in fourth grade, everything changed. Suddenly it was all about who's popular and who's not and if you're wearing the right thing. Which I never am. Ever.

The bus wheezes to a stop in front of the Bullet Hole House. It's called the Bullet Hole House even though the Anderson family owns it because two hundred and fifty years ago during the Revolutionary War, a retreating redcoat—that's what they use to call British soldiers—fired at it. Well, at Elisha Jones, who lived in the house back then. He was a minuteman and he'd accidentally slept through the

Heather Vogel Frederick

skirmish across the street at the Old North Bridge. He was standing there in his doorway watching the British retreat when it happened. Sometimes I think about the Jones family, who were probably sitting at their breakfast table when *wham!*—all of a sudden a bullet hits the house. I'd have been scared to death. At least it missed Elisha.

Anyway, the hole is still there and there's a little sign explaining all about it. The Bullet Hole House is on all the maps of Concord, and tourists are always stopping to take pictures of it. They take pictures of everything in our town. You can't turn around in Concord, Massachusetts, without bumping into history, my dad says, and I guess he's right.

The front door opens and someone runs out, but it isn't a minuteman and it isn't a redcoat, it's only Kyle Anderson. He swats me on the head as he passes my seat. It's more of a big brother swat than a mean swat, though. I've known Kyle since I was in diapers.

"Hey, Emma," he says.

"Hey, Kyle."

Behind me, Becca and Ashley chorus their hellos too, but Kyle ignores them and takes a seat beside my brother. Kyle and Darcy are best friends.

The bus lumbers on, round white-steepled Monument Square and on past Sleepy Hollow Cemetery, where all the famous people of Concord are buried, patriots and soldiers and writers like Henry David Thoreau and Ralph Waldo Emerson and Nathaniel Hawthorne and Louisa May Alcott. As we swing onto Old Bedford Road, the final leg of the bus ride to Walden Middle School, I start to feel sick. The butter-flies in my stomach feel more like a herd of buffalo, and I'm worried I might throw up like I did the first day of kindergarten. My mother loves to tell the story of how when she dropped me off in the class-room that day, my teacher leaned down to say hello, and I was so nerv-ous I threw up all over her shoes. "Emma really made a splash," is my mother's punchline. It always gets a laugh.

I don't feel like laughing now, though. I close my eyes and breathe deeply, trying to calm the stampeding buffalo. I can only imagine the impression I'll make on my first day of middle school if I walk into the classroom and barf.

It doesn't help that I can hear Becca and Ashley whispering about my skirt again. I feel my face grow hot and I wish for the millionth time that my mother hadn't made me wear it. It's pretty and every-thing, and nearly brand-new, but still, it's a hand-me-down. My mother said it looked fine and that no one would ever know, but I knew better.

The bus slows as we reach Half Moon Farm, but there are no Delaneys at the bus stop except Jess's dog Sugar, looking mournful, so we keep going. Jess's mom always drives her and her brothers on the first day of school. Her dad must have decided to keep up the family tradition this year. I wish he hadn't. Not that Jess could make Becca and Ashley any nicer—that would take complete personality transplants—but it always makes me feel better having my best friend around.

Heather Vogel Frederick

Trying to block out their comments, I concentrate on my poem again. I'm working on finding a good rhyme for "grape" (ape? cape? tape?) when we pull up in front of the middle school.

Mom made Darcy promise to take care of me this morning, and he herds me confidently through the crowded lobby. Everybody's pushing and shoving as they crowd around the lists posted on the wall by the office. Darcy runs his finger down the sixth grade homerooms and jabs at my name when he spots it.

"Miss Morales, 6-C," he says. I must look panicked because he smiles at me and pats my shoulder. Darcy's pretty nice, for a brother. "Don't worry," he tells me. "You'll like her."

"How about Jess?"

He looks at the list again, then shakes his head. "Sorry, Em—she's in 6-B with Mr. Flanagan. But he's a good dude too."

As Darcy steers me down the hall toward 6-C, I console myself with the thought that Jess and I will still probably see each other for most of our classes. We're both in all the advanced groups.

"Have fun!" my brother says, leaving me at my homeroom door.

I nod weakly, still feeling nauseous. No one pays me the slightest bit of attention as I walk in. They're all too busy looking for their name tags. I circle the desks nervously, hunting for mine. Great. Miss Morales put me right across from Megan Wong. I slip into my seat and slant a quick glance at her. Megan is flipping her perfect, shoulder-length black hair around and showing off her new earrings to Ashley and Becca. She must have gotten her ears pierced over summer vacation.

Jen Webster arrives and comes over to join them. The four of them travel in a pack, like wolves. The Fab Four, Darcy calls them. They like it when he says that. That's because they like my brother. Darcy's a jock, and the girls all think he's cute and call our house all the time to talk to him. Darcy and I both have the same short, curly brown hair and brown eyes, but so far, nobody thinks I'm cute.

"You're just a late bloomer," my mother tells me. "Be patient." This is mom-code for "My daughter is an ugly duckling and I'm hoping she'll turn out to be a swan," but still, it's comforting to hear. Especially when you don't see so much as a single swan feather yet when you look in the mirror.

I watch the Fab Four surreptitiously while I unpack my school supplies and organize my desk. Becca Chadwick is the queen bee. I learned this from a book my mother was reading over the summer about adolescent girls. She's a librarian and she's always reading books to try and understand me and my brother better.

Queen bees are the ones who end up being the boss. How this works, I have no idea, but every group has one. They're popular and stuck-up and they aren't generally very nice to the regular bees. That's certainly true for Becca Chadwick. And for Megan and Ashley and Jen, too. The three of them are like the queen bee's court—"wannabees," Jess and I call them.

The sad thing is that Megan Wong used to be my friend. Almost as good a friend as Jess. We used to play Barbies for hours after school in her sunroom. Megan made the most amazing clothes for them. I still

Heather Vogel Frederick

have some of the little dresses and hats and things that she sewed. Then in fourth grade I got glasses and Megan's father invented some computer gizmo and made a bazillion dollars, and that was the end of that. Now Megan's all rich and conceited. The sunroom is long gone— her family traded the cozy condo it belonged to for a house that looks like a museum. Or an airplane hangar. And Megan traded me for Becca, Ashley, and Jen.

Someone slides into the seat beside me. I look over. It's Zach Norton. His hair is bleached streaky blond from the sun and he smells like summer. The buffalo start thundering in my stomach again.

"Hi," I manage to whisper.

"Hey, Emma," he replies casually, then turns away and starts throwing wadded up balls of paper at Ethan MacDonald. Ethan bats them back at him with a ruler. The Fab Four are practically shrieking with laughter at something Megan just said, trying to get Zach's attention, but he doesn't notice. He's too busy with his baseball game. Why is it that girls think boys will notice them if they're loud, anyway?

I stare at the back of Zach's neck. He obviously just got a haircut, because there's a slim line of white skin between where his tan stops and where the edge of his sun-bleached hair begins, like the curl of surf against a sandy beach. I contemplate it for a while, then look around the room feeling a little better. Even if he ignores me all year, I'm still sitting next to Zach Norton. Things could be a whole lot worse. I could have been stuck at a desk beside Cassidy Sloane, for instance. She's new—she moved here from California at the end of fifth grade—and her mom used to be a fashion model, but you'd never know it by looking at Cassidy. She has red hair she never combs and scabby knees, and all she thinks about is sports, sports, sports.

"How about those Red Sox!" Zach yells over at her, and Cassidy grins and gives him a thumbs-up. The two of them played together on the same Little League team over the summer. I know this because they used to practice right before my brother Darcy's team. Sometimes I'd ride my bike over early just so I could watch Zach. Not that anyone ever suspected, of course. They all thought I was there to watch Darcy.

I get up to sharpen my pencil and make a mental note to start following the Red Sox so I'll have something to talk about with Zach. On the way back to my desk, I notice Megan staring at my skirt.

"Nicole Patterson had a skirt just like that last year," she says. "I wonder what she did with it?"

Becca and Ashley and Jen all snicker, right on cue. They're like one another's own personal laugh track. I feel my face turning hot with humiliation. The Pattersons go to our church. Nicole is an eighth grader like my brother, and her parents are always loading bags of her hand-me-downs into our station wagon after Sunday School. My mother says it's wonderfully generous of them and a big help to our family budget, but I'd give anything not to have to wear Nicole's rejects.

The rest of the day goes pretty much downhill from there, with the Fab Four needling me every opportunity they get. I'm close to tears by the time the last class rolls around. Thankfully, none of them are in the advanced group for science.

Heather Vogel Frederick

Science is okay. Nobody I know really loves it except Jess and Kevin Mullins, who skipped about four grades and is, like, eight, and will probably be accepted at Harvard before the rest of us even start high school. Jess loves it, of course. She would—she's a total brainiac. I'm smart enough, especially at reading and writing, but Jess is a *genius*. And if truth be told, a bit of a nerd. She took the math part of the SAT last spring—for fun. Who takes the SAT for fun? When they're not even twelve yet?

Our science teacher, Mr. Reed, passes around a bunch of handouts and then launches into a speech about the joys of middle school science.

"This year one of the exciting things we'll be doing is dissecting cow eyes," he tells us in the kind of voice usually reserved for telling your family you're taking them to Disney World.

I tug on Jess's braid to get her to look over her shoulder at me— she has the most amazingly gorgeous thick blonde hair, which she wears in a braid down her back—and when she does I roll my eyes and moo quietly. Jess giggles. Mr. Reed drones on, and I'm yawning like crazy when the bell finally rings and school is over.

Outside, Mr. Delaney is waiting in the pickup to take us home. Mrs. Delaney always used to do this, but she's away right now. We stop for ice cream to celebrate (celebrate what? not barfing at school? not crying in front of the Fab Four?), then head back to Half Moon Farm. Jess's dad drops us at the end of the driveway.

"I'll be back in a bit," he tells us. "I have to pick up the twins." Dylan and Ryan, Jess's little brothers, are first graders at Emerson Elementary. "Don't forget, you have a voice lesson in an hour, Jess."

Jess makes a face as her father drives away. "I hate voice lessons," she grumbles.

"Why?" I ask. Jess adores music, and she has the voice of an angel. She lifts a shoulder in a half shrug. "I don't know, I just do."

Jess never used to take voice lessons before her mother went away. A luxury farmers can't afford, Mr. Delaney always said. I guess organic farming isn't exactly the best-paying job in the world. Delaneys have owned Half Moon Farm for generations, but it was Jess's dad who decided to make it all-organic. He plows the fields with a pair of big Belgian draft horses named Led and Zep—after his favorite rock group, Led Zeppelin.

The Delaneys have chickens for fresh eggs and goats for milk and cheese and an apple orchard for fruit and pies, and depending on the season they sell all kinds of fresh herbs and berries and vegetables. Jess and I always help out at the farm stand in the summer. It's fun.

Anyway, now that Mrs. Delaney has this new job as an actress, I guess she's making lots of money and sending some of it home for luxuries like voice lessons.

Inside the house, we each grab an apple off the kitchen counter. Jess shoos Dolly Parton back outside. Not the country singer—a chicken. Mrs. Delaney loves country music, and she named all of the hens after her favorite stars. Sometimes they sneak into the house if somebody forgets to latch the back screen door. It's pretty funny to see

Heather Vogel Frederick

them wandering around. Once Patsy Cline hopped up on the sofa beside us and laid an egg. Jess and I about died laughing.

"Hey, it's three thirty," I tell Jess, glancing at the clock over the stove.

We take our backpacks up to her room. Sugar, Jess's Shetland sheepdog, is close on our heels. Jess flips on the TV.

"Hi, Mom!" she says, as her mother's face appears on the screen.

I wave. "Hi, Mrs. Delaney!"

Sugar barks.

Jess's mom is on a soap opera called *HeartBeats*. She went to New York out of the blue last month to audition, and she got the part. She found an apartment and she's living there for now. I'm not really sure when she's planning to come back home. Jess doesn't like to talk about it much, but she watches her mother's show every day.

"Her hair looks good like that," I say.

Jess nods and takes a bite of her apple.

Sugar barks at the TV screen again as Jess's mother starts talking to the actress who plays her best friend. Sugar misses Mrs. Delaney too. And her sister. The Delaneys actually have two shelties—Sugar and Spice. Mr. Delaney got them for Jess and her mother for Valentine's Day a couple of years ago. They were the most adorable puppies I've ever seen. Mrs. Delaney took Spice to New York with her to keep her from getting lonely.

After a while we turn the volume down. The dialogue on *HeartBeats* is unbelievably lame. I don't know how Jess's mother can keep her face straight when she says her lines. Honestly, I could write better stuff than that.

"Help me with my math homework?" I ask Jess.

"Sure," she replies. Jess has skipped ahead to algebra this year, with Darcy and Kyle. I'm in regular sixth grade math. I'm terrible at it. Jess has been my tutor since, like, kindergarten.

Keeping an occasional eye on the TV screen, we do our homework together, and by the time we're finished Mr. Delaney is back and ready to take Jess to her voice lesson. He drops me off at home on the way.

"See you tomorrow!" Jess calls out the window.

"See you!" I call back, and go inside.

My dad is just putting dinner on the table. He does all the cooking in our family. He says it's easier this way because he works at home, but I think it's self-defense. My mother is a terrible cook. She admits it, too. She says she can't even boil water.

"So, how was your first day back at school?" my father asks as we take our seats.

"Great!" says Darcy.

"Okay, I guess," I mumble.

My mother looks at me sharply. "Just okay?"

I shrug.

"Maybe some comfort food will help," says my father, passing me a plate heaped with his special homemade meat loaf and mashed potatoes.

"Better give me some of that too," says my mother. "I had a meeting with the head of the library board this afternoon."

Heather Vogel Frederick

"Calliope Chadwick?" my father replies, serving her up an extra-generous helping. "And how is the wasp and her colossal bottom?"

"Nicholas Hawthorne!" my mother scolds. "Little pitchers!"

That's little pitchers as in "Little pitchers have big ears." In other words, Darcy and me. My father looks over at us. He grins. We grin back. Calliope Chadwick's sharp tongue and extra-large backside are well-known around Concord.

"You object to my use of the word 'colossal'?" my dad says to my mother, the picture of innocence. "You would prefer, perhaps, 'gargantuan'?"

"How about 'enormous'?" offers Darcy.

"'Vast'?" I suggest, feeling a twinge of guilt for poking fun at Mrs. Chadwick. I'm short, but I'm not exactly what you'd call petite myself.

"'Immense'?" counters my brother.

"Enough!" cries my mother, trying to suppress her laughter. The synonym game is a time-honored Hawthorne family tradition. She looks around the table at us, shaking her head. "Honestly, what am I going to do with you three? You are incorrigible. And, Nicholas, you're the worst offender. We're supposed to be teaching our children to respect their elders!"

"We *are* teaching them to respect their elders," my dad says cheerfully. "Those that are worthy of respect. It's no secret that Calliope Chadwick has a shrewish temper, and there's no point pretending we can't all see her massive—"

My mother holds up both hands. "Cease and desist!"

My father smoothly changes the subject. "Did I tell you that the Boston *Post* sent me a new Austen biography to review?"

All thoughts of the Chadwick posterior fly instantly out of my mother's head. "Is it any good?" she replies, her eyes lighting up with excitement. "Can I read it when you're done? Can I read it first?"

Books are my parents' life. My mom is a librarian at the Concord Public Library, and my dad's a freelance writer. Not surprisingly, books are a frequent topic of discussion around our house.

Particularly books by Jane Austen. My mother is an Austen nut. She even named my brother and me after characters in her favorite Jane Austen novels. It's a good thing my brother is as popular as he is, because a name like Darcy could get him in a whole lot of trouble otherwise. But nobody at school teases my brother about much of anything. First of all, everybody likes him, and second of all, he's six feet tall already and a lineman on the football team. And captain of the middle school hockey team two years in a row now, and as if that weren't enough, he's an All-Star baseball pitcher to boot. The high school coaches are practically drooling at the thought of getting him on their teams next year.

It's not until dessert (chocolate pudding—more "comfort food") that the subject of Mrs. Chadwick comes up again.

"So tonight's the big night for you two girls, right?" my dad asks, gazing at my mother and me.

I give him a blank look. My mother smiles that smile she pulls out when she's up to something. The one that makes her look just like

Melville our cat after he's made a successful raid on the bird feeder.

"That's right," she says. "Although if Calliope has her way, it may not get off the ground."

My dad takes a bite of pudding. "How did she find out? Is she in your yoga class?"

"No, though it would doubtless do her some good." My mother bites her lip at this uncharitable slip, then continues primly, "She's objecting on the grounds that the library charter forbids private clubs from meeting on public property, but I think it's because she's miffed at the member list."

My eyes are bouncing from one of them to the other like a spectator at a tennis match. I'm completely clueless here.

"Well, don't let it spoil your big night," my father says.

"What big night?" I ask suspiciously.

My mother turns to me. "I have a little surprise for you," she tells me. "After yoga class, some of the other mothers and I were talking—"

"Uh-oh," I say. I can't help it. "Some of the other mothers and I were talking" is mom-code for "You're not going to like what's coming next."

My mother sighs. "Don't look at me like that, Emma," she says. "You haven't even heard what I'm going to say."

It doesn't matter. Whatever it is, I know for sure I won't like it. Last time my mother started a sentence that way, I ended up in ballet class. Talk about total humiliation. People built like me are not meant to wear leotards. We're maybe meant to bring in the harvest or something. The time before that, I got to volunteer at a local animal shelter, which wasn't so bad until that windbag of a parrot nearly bit off my finger. I could go on—the list is endless.

My mother ignores my expression. "We've decided to start a mother-daughter book club," she says in her best Mrs. Hawthorne-the-librarian voice, "and tonight's our first meeting. Won't that be fun?"

Darcy groans. He looks over at my father. "Man, Dad, am I glad you don't do yoga."

I stare at my mother. I must look like she's just informed me that she's planning to shave both our heads, because she bursts out laughing.

"Come on, Emma, it's not *that* bad," she says.

"Who else is going to be there?" I demand, suddenly putting two and two together and getting four, for once. "Did Mrs. Chadwick make you invite Becca?"

My mother smiles her sly, catlike smile again. "You'll have to wait and see," she tells me loftily. "Don't worry—it's going to be great, I promise."

But I know better. It's just like Nicole Patterson's hand-me-downs. It's not going to be great at all. It's going to be a disaster.

Heather Vogel Frederick

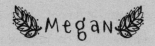

Megan

"Conceit spoils the finest genius."

"You can go shopping anytime," my mother tells me.

I don't answer. Instead, I pull my cell phone out of my purse and take a picture of my face—mad—and send it to Becca. Then I text her: CAN U BELIEVE IT?

NO, she texts back. I CAN'T!

Becca's mother was going to drive us to the mall tonight to celebrate our first day of middle school, but now I can't go. My stupid mother's signed us up for some stupid book club without even asking me!

"By the way, honey, that catalogue came today," she says, turning into the parking lot across the street from the library. "Remember? The one I told you about? For the science-and-math camp in New Hampshire next summer?" She reaches over and pats my hand. I pull it away. I have no interest in going to science-and-math camp, and she knows it.

"High school is just around the corner for you now, Megan," she continues blithely. "Your skills could definitely use a boost, especially if you want to get into Colonial Academy."

I glance past the library at the line of stately white buildings that house our town's famous private school. I have even less interest in attending Colonial Academy than I do in going to science-and-math camp. "Forget it, Mom. I don't want—"

She pats my hand again. "You're too young to know what you want, sweetie. That's what your father and I are here for. We only want what's best for you."

What's best for me? My parents don't know what's best for me—they don't even *see* me! Especially my mother. She's too busy with all her causes and charities. "Why do we even have to talk about this now?" I grumble. "I'm only in the sixth grade, for Pete's sake."

"It's never too soon to think about your future," my mother replies. "You're going to make a difference in this world, Megan. You'll do something unselfish and grand—study environmental law, maybe. And this mother-daughter book club will look great on your application to the academy."

I give her a withering look, which she ignores.

As usual, my mother hears what she wants to hear, and sees what she wants to see. When she looks at me, she must see some other girl she wishes she had for a daughter—one that's more like the stereotype. You know, studious Chinese-American girl who's a whiz at math and science. Instead, she's stuck with just plain me, Megan Rose Wong. Who likes to hang out at the mall and shop and who wants to be a fashion designer someday, not go to MIT like she and Dad did.

Heather Vogel Frederick

My mother and I are like night and day. The only thing we have in common is our hair color. But she wears hers cut short, in a no-nonsense style that isn't very flattering. She never wears makeup, and her clothes—it's not like she can't afford nice things, for Pete's sake! But no, it's yoga pants and T-shirts with slogans like "Save the Rain Forest" on them, made only of natural fibers of course. My mother's life is dedicated to improving the world.

The Hawthornes pull into the parking space beside us. They're driving the same tin can they've had since Emma and I were in kinder-garten. I'll bet it still smells like moldy french fries. Emma and I used to sit in the backseat after swim lessons at Walden Pond and stuff them down into the seatbelt slots, until her mom caught us and threatened not to buy us any more kids' meals at the drive-thru if we didn't quit it.

Just then Zach and Ethan and Third—his real name is Cranfield Bartlett III, but everybody calls him Third—swoosh by on their bikes. I open my door quickly and hop out so they'll see me, glad that I wore my yellow sundress and even more glad that we're not driving the Hawthornes' old beater. I would be embarrassed to death to be seen in that thing.

The boys spot me and loop around the parking lot once to show off. I wave casually, like I don't care. They all grin and wave back, then pedal furiously away. Zach glances back over his shoulder one last time before they disappear out of the parking lot. I think he likes me.

Beside me, Emma has gotten out of her car too, and I see her staring after Zach. Fat chance. Emma Hawthorne doesn't understand the first thing about boys. The outfits she wears! She's worse than my mother. Tonight, for instance, she's wearing shorts, which at her weight are not flattering, and ratty flip-flops, and her T-shirt, which I'm sure used to be Nicole Patterson's, has some sort of stain on it. Chocolate pudding, maybe?

"Hi, Megan!" says Mrs. Hawthorne, all cheery.

I grunt in reply, not cheery at all.

My mother clamps her hand down on my shoulder. "Manners," she whispers through teeth tightly clenched in a smile.

"Mom!" I protest, trying to squirm out of her death grip, then give up and turn back toward Mrs. Hawthorne. "Hi, Mrs. H."

"Glad you two could come," Emma's mom replies, winking at my mom. "New car, Lily?"

My mother nods proudly. "It's a hybrid. Environmentally friendly, you know, and great on the gas mileage."

I feel her death grip relax, and she prods me forward across the street. Inside, we stop at the main desk to say hello to the library staff. They all know my mother. Everybody in town knows my mother. She's on the library's board of trustees, and on the board of just about everything else in Concord. My mother, the charity queen. Ever since my dad sold his invention, she's been on some kind of campaign to give his money away. It's like she feels guilty about it or something.

Mrs. Hawthorne leads us into a conference room. A window at the far end overlooks the children's section. Emma and I exchange a hasty

Heather Vogel Frederick

glance. We used to go there every week for story hour when we were little. I remember how much I used to look forward to it. But that was a long time ago.

I take a seat at the table beside my mother and wonder who else is coming tonight. A second later, the door bangs open and I get my answer as Cassidy Sloane stumps into the room. She glares at us and slams herself into a chair. I'm guessing she doesn't want to be here either.

Her mother is right behind her. "Hi, everybody," she says with a weary smile.

My mother smiles back. She's probably happy to see that there's somebody in this world with worse manners than mine. "Hi, Clementine!"

Mrs. Sloane is gorgeous. She used to be a fashion model—a really famous one, the kind who's known just by her first name. Her face was on the cover of all the top magazines. She still looks like a model. She's tall and slender with long blonde hair, and she wears the most amazing clothes. I try not to stare, but I can't help it. Her short skirt and T-shirt look casual but I know they're both designer and probably cost a fortune. Her high-heeled sandals show off a perfect pedicure, and she's accessorized with big hoop earrings and a jangle of silver bracelets.

I'm tempted to take out my sketchbook and draw her, but I don't. My mother would have a cow if she saw my sketchbook, especially after our argument in the car. She hates my sketchbook. She thinks fashion is selfish and stupid. "Frivolous," she calls it. Now if I designed outfits for the homeless, she'd probably think it was okay. An acceptable hobby to pursue in my spare time, after I go to MIT and Harvard Law School and become Super Megan and help save the planet.

"We'll wait just a few more minutes before we start," says Mrs. Hawthorne, with a nod at the last two empty chairs.

We're all quiet for a bit. Cassidy scuffs her feet on the floor, back and forth, back and forth, like an angry metronome. I look at her and her mother curiously. How does a knockout like Clementine Sloane produce a freak like Cassidy? At least my mother and I look similar on the outside. Except for the fact that they're both tall, Cassidy and her mother look like they come from different planets. Why doesn't Mrs. Sloane at least fix her up a little? Cassidy is plain as a broomstick, with long skinny legs and ratty red hair whose bangs look like she cut them herself with nail scissors. In the dark. And her fashion sense is even more hopeless than Emma's. I stare at her gym shorts and faded Red Sox T-shirt. I can't believe she shares the same DNA with the world-famous *Clementine*.

Apparently, neither can her mother. Every time Mrs. Sloane looks at Cassidy a pleat of wrinkles appears between her eyebrows.

The door opens again and Emma's face lights up. I look over and practically fall out of my chair when I see Jessica Delaney and her father. They invited *Goat Girl* to join this club? The faint odor of manure wafts in with the Delaneys, and there is an honest-to-gosh piece of hay stuck in Jess's long blonde braid. Unbelievable!

Mr. Delaney hands my mother an egg carton and she slips him

Heather Vogel Frederick

some money. The Delaneys own an organic farm on the edge of town and my mother buys all our produce from them. Anything organic, my mother will buy it. The environment thing again.

Goat Girl gives us all a shy glance and sits down beside Emma. Jess Delaney is about the weirdest person I know. She's been weird forever. In kindergarten she brought her bug collection for show-and-tell, and she knew all their Latin names and everything. And she actually likes math and science. Maybe my mother can send her to that camp in New Hampshire instead of me.

"Welcome, Jess," Mrs. Hawthorne says warmly.

Jess doesn't reply, of course. She just looks down at the table. She hardly ever says a word. It's like she's mute or something. About the only person she talks to is Emma. She's gotten even quieter since her mother left for New York. Not that anyone could blame Mrs. Delaney—that farm they live on is disgusting. We stopped by to pick up some eggs once and there were actual live chickens walking around in the kitchen. Jess's mother probably got tired of having to share her house with livestock.

"There's a chair for you, too, Michael," says Mrs. Hawthorne, gesturing to the seat beside Jess.

Jess's father has a kind of dazed expression on his face, like he was abducted by aliens. My mother says that everyone who has twins looks like that. Jess has two little five-year-old brothers who are even more repulsive than she is. Mr. Delaney shoves his hands (grimy) into the pockets of his jeans (also grimy). "The boys are waiting in the truck," he says, adding awkwardly, "Besides, I thought this was girls-only."

Mrs. Hawthorne laughs. "In your case, we'd be happy to make an exception. The main point of the club is for parents and daughters to share some quality time together."

Mr. Delaney nods. "I'll think about it," he says. "But I don't know if it's my cup of tea."

"Well, the door is always open," Mrs. Hawthorne tells him. "Feel free to join us any time."

Mr. Delaney leaves and Jess looks anxiously at the empty chair beside her. Mrs. Hawthorne gets up and whisks it away.

"As you know, girls," she says brightly, taking her seat again, "we moms got to talking after yoga class a few weeks ago and decided that we wanted to do something special with you this year. Something more grown-up, now that you're in middle school. Mrs. Sloane came up with the idea of a mother-daughter book club, and we all agreed that it was the perfect thing."

She and Mrs. Sloane and my mother all beam at us like they've just won the Nobel Prize or something. None of us beam back.

Mrs. Sloane rummages in her big leather bag, which is the exact same pink as her fingernails and toenails and very expensive-looking. I automatically reach for my sketchbook again, but stop myself just in time. Instead, I try and memorize the bag's design and make a mental note to myself to add purses to my first fashion line.

Mrs. Sloane pulls out a paperback and holds it up. "The first book we're going to read together is *Little Women* by Louisa May Alcott."

Cassidy groans. I start to groan too, but stop because my mother is giving me the look. The one that says don't you dare, not if you want to live. The evil-witch-mother eye of death, my dad calls it.

I pull out my cell phone instead and text Becca again: LAME LAME LAME! GOAT GIRL IS HERE. P-U. WE HAVE TO READ LITTLE WOMEN. I think about snapping a picture of Jess but add a frowny face instead and press send.

My mother reaches over and plucks the phone out of my hand. I start to protest, but she gives me the look again.

Mrs. Sloane continues, "We thought that since Louisa lived right here in town and wrote the book at Orchard House and is such a famous Concord author and everything, *Little Women* would be the perfect choice to kick off our new club."

"You've got to be joking!" Cassidy takes the book from her mother and hefts it like a dumbbell. "This sucker is huge!" She riffles through the pages and looks up in disbelief. "It's over seven hundred pages long!"

Mrs. Hawthorne laughs. "It *is* a long book, Cassidy, you're right. But I think you'll find it's a good one. And don't worry, we've got all year to read it."

My mouth drops open. A whole *year*? I turn and stare at my mother. I shake my head, *No way.* She nods and smiles, *Yes way.* We communicate like this sometimes, without words.

"How am I supposed to have time to read this thing plus do my homework plus skate?" Cassidy demands.

"I didn't know you were a skater, Cassidy!" gushes my mother, flicking me a glance. "Figure skating is such a lovely sport."

Yet another of my mother's major disappointments in life is that I quit figure skating. For a while there, before she decided I should become an environmental lawyer, she had plans for me to be the next Michelle Kwan.

"Are you taking lessons with Eva Bergson?" my mother continues. Eva Bergson is one of Concord's most famous residents. Almost as famous as Louisa May Alcott. She won a gold medal in the Olympics about a hundred years ago, and now she runs a skating school.

"I play hockey," Cassidy says flatly.

"There's no need to be rude," scolds Mrs. Sloane. She turns to my mother. "You'll have to excuse her, Lily," she says apologetically. "Cassidy played on a girls' team in California, and I'm afraid she was terribly disappointed to find that there isn't one at the middle school here in Concord."

"What about the Merrimac League?" asks Mrs. Hawthorne.

Mrs. Sloane shakes her head ruefully. "I looked into it but the commitment is way too intense for a single mother like me—all those practices, national tournaments, travel. There's no way I could swing that."

Cassidy shoots her a sour look.

"And classes with Eva?"

"Cassidy's not interested, and Eva's all booked up anyway," Mrs. Sloane tells her.

My mother whips her planner out of her purse and jots down a note to herself. "I'm co-chairing the new rec center fundraiser with

Heather Vogel Frederick

Eva," she tells Mrs. Sloane. "I'll put in a good word for you, if you'd like. She's a marvelous teacher." She smiles at Cassidy, who folds her arms defiantly across her chest.

"I play hockey," she repeats.

"Well," says Mrs. Hawthorne smoothly. "Let's get started, shall we? Since we obviously haven't read any of the book yet, I thought that tonight we'd talk about the club rules and learn a few fun facts about Louisa, then go out for ice cream."

I slouch down in my chair. This is getting worse by the minute. Ice cream? What if someone from school sees all of us together? They'll think we're friends. What if Zach Norton is there?

The door to the conference room flies open and Becca Chadwick's mother barges in. She has brown hair like Mrs. Hawthorne, but unlike Emma's mother, who wears hers in a ponytail, Mrs. Chadwick's is styled into one of those poufy bouffants that looks sort of like a football helmet. Her eyes are blue, like Becca's, but much paler. Pale as robins' eggs, but piercing, which is a weird combination.

"Aha!" she says, looking at Mrs. Hawthorne accusingly. "Caught you! I thought I made myself quite clear this afternoon, Phoebe. No exclusive clubs are allowed to meet on public property."

Mrs. Hawthorne sighs. "Calliope, for one thing, we're not exclusive, just private. And for another, I couldn't change our meeting place on such short notice. We were just about to take a vote on a new location and then we'll be leaving, I promise you."

Mrs. Chadwick's sour expression softens when she spots me. "So sorry you can't join the girls and me tonight, Megan. I know Becca is disappointed." She glares at my mother. "But apparently SOME people prefer to let their daughters join EXCLUSIVE CLUBS instead of engaging in wholesome recreational activities with their dearest FRIENDS!"

She looks around the table dismissively at Emma and Jess and Cassidy, who she clearly feels don't fall into this category. I can't say I disagree.

My mother presses her lips together firmly and doesn't reply. My mother doesn't like Mrs. Chadwick. Actually, most people in Concord don't like Mrs. Chadwick, on account of her temper. My father calls her "the snapping turtle."

With a final sniff of disapproval, Mrs. Chadwick waddles out.

My mother looks ruefully at Mrs. Hawthorne. "Maybe we should have invited—"

"No," Emma's mother says firmly. "We have every right to form a group of our own choosing. And Calliope has no right to try and make us feel guilty."

"Should we vote about where we want to meet?" asks Mrs. Sloane.

How about nowhere, I want to say, but don't.

"We could take turns hosting the meetings at our homes," says Mrs. Hawthorne. "Or if you'd all prefer, I can reserve a room at the Arts Center."

"No, let's meet in our homes," says Cassidy's mother. "It's cozier that way."

Heather Vogel Frederick

The mothers all nod in agreement.

"Girls?" asks Mrs. Hawthorne.

None of us say a word. Emma gives a half shrug.

"I'll take that as a yes," her mother says briskly. "It's settled. We'll take turns hosting."

Jess Delaney gets that anxious look on her face again. Mrs. Hawthorne gives her shoulder an encouraging pat. "Of course, if someone is unable to host for any reason, that's not a problem."

"I volunteer for next month," says Mrs. Sloane.

Cassidy glares at her. Mrs. Hawthorne passes out rose-patterned folders. "THE MOTHER-DAUGHTER BOOK CLUB" is written on each one in fancy calligraphy. Cassidy holds hers gingerly between her thumb and forefinger. She looks like she's been handed a dead cat.

"This is to keep your handouts in," explains Mrs. Hawthorne. "And here's your first one."

At the top is printed "RULES FOR THE MOTHER-DAUGHTER BOOK CLUB," followed by a long list. We go over it quickly. Finish each month's assigned reading. Come prepared to discuss the questions. Respect your fellow club members. Don't interrupt. Be positive and supportive of one another's ideas. Blah, blah, blah.

Mrs. Hawthorne passes out two more sheets of paper. "This is your assignment for October's meeting, plus a little information about the author."

I scan the assignment. Six chapters a month? Forget it! I stuff it inside my folder along with the club rules and look at the next sheet.

FUN FACTS ABOUT LOUISA

1. Louisa May Alcott was born in 1832.

2. She had three sisters, and loosely based *Little Women* on her own family. Bronson and Abba Alcott, her parents, became Mr. and Mrs. March. Her older sister Anna became the character Meg, Louisa herself was Jo, May was Amy, and Elizabeth ("Lizzie") was Beth.

3. *Little Women* was originally written as two books, but over the years the volumes were combined. It's been translated into many languages around the world and has also been performed as a stage play and a musical. At least six movie versions of the story have been made.

"Why don't we just watch one of the movies instead?" suggests Cassidy. "This dumb book is way too long."

"The whole point is to spend time reading together, honey," says her mother with a pained smile. "It wouldn't hurt you to do something cultured once in a while, something ladylike."

Cassidy gives a very unladylike grunt in reply.

Mrs. Hawthorne stands up. "So, are we ready to go to Kimball Farm?"

Beside me, Emma perks up. "Likes to eat" would be at the top of any "Fun Facts About Emma Hawthorne" list. Not that I mind a trip to

Heather Vogel Frederick

Kimball Farm. They have the best strawberry ice cream in the world. But the idea of going there with this group is enough to make anyone lose their appetite.

Out in the car, my mother fastens her seatbelt, humming happily to herself. "Such nice girls," she says. "This is going to be fun. Don't you think so?"

I look over at her and shake my head. Fun? She's got to be kidding. Going to the mall with Becca and Ashley and Jen would have been fun. But I don't say a word. Instead, I promise myself I will find a way out. There's no way I'm staying in a book club with Emma Hawthorne and Cassidy Sloane and Goat Girl. No way at all.

CASSIDY

"A quick temper, sharp tongue, and restless spirit
were always getting her into scrapes . . ."

I fling open the front door. It bangs against the wall, announcing my arrival.

"Hi, honey!" my mother calls from the kitchen.

I shrug my backpack onto the entry hall bench and glance over at the grandfather clock opposite. It's three fifteen. If I hustle, I can grab some ice time before our dumb book club meeting. It's here at my house tonight. Right before the party.

My mother appears, carrying a platter of cupcakes. They're covered with orange frosting and decorated with licorice to look like little jack-o'-lanterns. "What do you think?" she asks.

"They look radioactive," I tell her, wrinkling my nose. It's true. Nothing in nature is that shade of orange except maybe some rare fungus.

She shoots me a look. "You don't have to be rude about it. I'm just trying to do something nice for you."

"Nice?" I snap. "Nice is not inviting my entire class to our house for a Halloween party without asking me first."

My mother sighs. "Honey, I'm just trying to help you make friends."

"I don't need your help." I open the hall closet and rummage noisily through my hockey equipment. My voice is as sharp as the blades on my skates, but I don't care. The book club was bad enough, but now this?

"I just thought, what with you being so disappointed about no hockey team here . . ." My mother's voice trails off.

I back out of the closet and turn to face her. "You're probably thrilled there isn't a team! You never wanted me to play anyway!"

A hurt expression creeps over her face. "That's not fair, Cassidy. It's not that I don't want you to play, it's just that it's dangerous and—"

"And what? Unladylike? Dad never cared about that."

My mother's eyes fill with tears at the mention of my father. Silently, she takes her cupcakes and retreats to the kitchen. The ruckus has brought my older sister Courtney down from her bedroom. She leans over the banister and glares at me.

"What's the matter with you?" she says. "Why do you always have to be so mean to Mom?"

"I wasn't trying to be mean!" I protest. "It's true—she doesn't want me to play hockey. She probably picked Concord on purpose when she found out they don't have a girls' team at the middle school!"

"That's ridiculous, and you know it," my sister scoffs. "You know as well as I do that we moved here to be near Nana and Grampie after Dad died."

Courtney is a sophomore in high school and thinks she knows everything. Her words make me squirm inwardly, though, because she's right. "You wouldn't understand," I say bitterly.

"Did it ever occur to you that it wasn't easy for Mom to leave California either? Maybe she's trying to make some new friends, too."

I gesture at the hallway, which is draped with fake cobwebs and spiders and stuff. "How, by making them think we're the Addams family?"

Courtney shakes her head in disgust. "Grow up, Cassidy." She disappears back upstairs. I sling my skates over my shoulder and head out the door to get my bike.

An hour on the ice clears my head. It always does. For once free skate is not too crowded and I fly up and down the rink, free as a bird, practicing crossovers and sprints and turns and working up a pretty good sweat in the process.

"Hey, you're not bad."

Startled, I skate to a stop and look up to see a tall boy with curly brown hair standing in front of me. It's Darcy Hawthorne, Emma's older brother. I recognize him from Little League.

"Thanks."

Darcy flicks me a smile and skates off. I watch him go. He's not bad either. Nice foot work, nice technique. Lucky, too. He's a boy, so he has a team to play on. As he sails down the ice, I feel a stab of envy. Life is so unfair! Hockey was what got me through those awful months after Dad died. And now I've lost it, too.

The shine's gone off my ice time. I stump away toward the benches to unlace my skates, and a few minutes later I'm on my bike heading home. As I turn down Walden Street toward Hubbard, I pass Zach and Ethan and Third sitting on the steps of the bank.

"See you tonight!" Zach shouts, and the black cloud hanging over me lifts a little. Maybe the party won't be so awful. Most of my baseball team will be there, and I can hang out with them.

But first I have to get through book club.

They're all clustered in the front hall when I arrive. My mom is talking with the other moms, and Megan and Emma and Jess are staring at the decorations. Piles and piles of decorations. Our house is practically encrusted with them. Tombstones line the staircase; huge black rubber tarantulas are scattered along the banister and the hallway bench; a family of vampires (mannequins dressed in black capes—who knows where Mom dug them up) is sitting at the dining room table, and absolutely everything is covered in fake cobwebs. When it comes to decorating for the holidays—any holiday—give my mother an inch and she'll take a mile.

"Hey, Cassidy," says Emma. She's in her costume already. I think she's a vegetable of some kind—an eggplant, maybe?

"Hey, Emma."

"I'm a Concord grape," she explains, noting my puzzled look. I nod. Unbelievably lame.

"How about you, Jess?" I ask, checking out her white lab coat and crazy white wig. "You look like your hair exploded."

She smiles shyly. "Albert Einstein," she whispers.

Megan Wong snorts. "Figures. You two will definitely win for stupidest costumes."

Jess's smile disappears, and Emma shifts uncomfortably in her green tights. I glare at Megan, but she ignores me and puts on more lip gloss. I knew girls like her back in California. Mean as snakes, for no reason.

"Cassidy, why don't you put your skates away and we'll get started," says my mother. "I thought we'd have our meeting in the turret." Her voice sounds overly cheery and I feel a prickle of guilt. Obviously, her feelings are still hurt.

"The turret? Cool!" Emma exclaims.

Megan rolls her eyes, which are heavily made up with blue eyeshadow. She's dressed as a pop singer, which means she looks pretty much the same way she does most days at school, only a little flashier.

My mother, who is dressed as a witch, complete with green face paint and a huge fake wart on her nose, leads the way upstairs. I throw my skates into the closet and follow. The turret is on the third floor of our Victorian house, off an attic that would have been my dad's study if he were still alive. Which he isn't.

"This is awesome!" Emma says as we all crowd into the circular room. She sighs. "I wish our house had a turret. You're so lucky, Cassidy."

Heather Vogel Frederick

"Lucky" is not the word I'd use to describe my life, but Emma's right about the turret. It is pretty awesome, even if it makes our house look like something out of a horror movie. My mom calls it her thinking room. There's a window seat that runs all the way around, and the windows above it are crisscrossed in little diamond shapes. Underneath the seat are bookcases filled with all our family photo albums, plus my mom's gardening and decorating and cooking books.

I would never in a million years tell my mother this, but sometimes I come up here when she's not around and look through our photo albums. She and my dad took zillions of pictures of us when we were little. Courtney looks just like my mom, blonde and perfect. I look like my dad. He had red hair too, and gray eyes like mine. It's been over a year since the accident, and I still can't look at his pictures without wanting to cry. Dad was the one who taught me how to skate, and catch a ball, and ride a bike, and surf, and do all the things I love to do. He was the best.

We take our seats. Mom doesn't look at me as she passes me my book club folder, and I feel that pang of guilt again.

"Before we start," says Mrs. Hawthorne, who is dressed as a scarecrow, "I have presents for everybody. They're from Jess's mom."

Jess looks surprised to hear this.

"I saw your mother on the cover of *TV Guide* yesterday at the supermarket checkout," Megan says. "That red dress was gorgeous."

Her mother elbows her. Megan flinches. "Ouch! What did you do that for?" she protests. "All I said was that she looked nice!"

I don't know the whole story with Jess's mom, just a few bits I overheard when Mrs. Hawthorne dropped by a few weeks ago for tea, after yoga class. I guess Mrs. Delaney moved to New York to be an actress, which is kind of a weird thing for a mother to do.

Mrs. Hawthorne hands us each a spiral-bound notebook. On the cover is a picture of four girls in old-fashioned dresses. One is sitting, and the other three are standing behind her.

"Oh, how lovely!" says my mother. She adores stuff like this. I hate it. Too girly.

"It's one of the Jessie Wilcox Smith illustrations from *Little Women*," says Mrs. Hawthorne. "It's the March sisters, see? Beth is sitting down, and behind her are Jo on the right, Meg in the middle, and Amy on the left. Shannon sent a card, too." She holds it out to Jess. "Would you like to read it aloud to us, sweetie?"

Jess shakes her head shyly.

"I'll read it then, shall I?" says Mrs. Hawthorne. She opens the card. "To my favorite 'little woman' and her friends: When I saw these in a shop here in Manhattan, I knew they were meant for you. I worked as a guide at Orchard House one summer during college, and I remember that the Alcotts all kept journals. I thought perhaps you might like to as well, as part of your club. You know the old saying, 'Preserve your memories, keep them well; what you forget, you can never retell.' Have fun! Wish I could be there!"

"Your mom is so thoughtful," Mrs. Wong says to Jess, her antennae wagging approvingly. She's dressed as a honey bee, and "Sweeten Your

Heather Vogel Frederick

Day Naturally!" is emblazoned on her black-and-yellow-striped tunic.

Mrs. Hawthorne passes the card to Jess, who fingers it quietly.

"Keeping journals is a splendid idea for our club," says Mrs. Hawthorne. "Did you know that the Alcott girls were required to share their journals with their family?"

"They had to let their *parents* read them?" Emma sounds horrified.

Mrs. Hawthorne nods. I swear she knows everything. It's probably because she's a librarian and gets to read all day.

"I know it must sound awful to you, but, remember, they grew up in a different era," she continues. "Bronson and Abba didn't do this to pry—they felt it was a good form of family communication. Their girls could express their thoughts and feelings, and they could write comments in response."

"I would just *die* if anybody ever read my journal!" cries Emma, clutching her new spiral-bound notebook to her grape costume. "Promise me you'll never read it, Mom."

"I promise," says Mrs. Hawthorne solemnly. "You know," she continues slowly, eyeing Jess, "Mr. Alcott was very shy as a young man."

Jess looks up. Mrs. Hawthorne smiles at her. "So shy, in fact, that the only way he could muster the courage to propose to Abba was by letting her read journal entries that he had written about his love for her."

I take my new journal and shove it under the cushion of the window seat. What a wimp! I will not be writing in my journal about anything, especially not love.

"So, did everyone do the reading?" asks my mother.

Emma's hand shoots up. I give her a scornful look. Teacher's pet.

"Can you tell us a bit about the first few chapters?"

"The book starts at Christmas," Emma replies. "Mr. March is away at war—the Civil War—and the girls are all sad because they don't have any money for presents."

I stare out the window as she talks. The delicious aroma of pizza drifts up from the kitchen. Courtney is downstairs getting set up for the party. Outside, dusk is falling fast and the littlest kids are already out trick-or-treating. A pair of tiny ghosts flit up our front path. I hear faint shrieks as they pass the jack-o'-lantern on the bottom of the porch steps. I smile. The jack-o-lantern was my idea. I bought it with my allowance downtown at Vanderhoof's Hardware. Dad would have loved it. He loved practical jokes. Once he put a six-foot-tall inflatable Godzilla in the bathroom, and when Mom went in there in the middle of the night her shrieks woke us all up. She wasn't too happy about it, but he thought it was hilarious. So did I. Anyway, the jack-o'-lantern is rigged with a motion detector, and whenever anyone walks by, it blinks its ember-red eyes and chuckles this evil chuckle. It sounds stupid, but it's really spooky if you aren't expecting it.

The ghosts are followed by a fairy princess, a miniature vampire, and a baby dressed in a dinosaur costume. The baby's father is pushing the stroller. My eyes suddenly mist over. Dad was always the one to take us trick-or-treating while Mom stayed home and handed out candy. I swipe at the tears angrily.

Heather Vogel Frederick

"Cassidy?"

"What?" My reply fires out like a slapshot, and Mrs. Hawthorne looks startled. Mom glares at me. "Sorry," I mumble. "I didn't hear the question."

"I asked what you think of the character Jo?"

I shrug. "She's okay, I guess." Actually, she's the only one of the March sisters I can stand at all. The others are way too prissy.

"She's quite a tomboy, isn't she? Does she remind you of anyone?"

My mother looks over at me and her face softens and her lips quirk up in a smile, the first one I've seen all day. The famous "Clementine" smile that launched a thousand magazine covers. The smile that will be paying for our college educations, as she often reminds Courtney and me.

"She definitely reminds me of Cassidy, if that's what you're hinting at, Phoebe," says Mrs. Wong.

I shrug again, but secretly I'm pleased.

We talk about the book some more, and come up with words that describe each of the other March sisters. We decide that Meg is "practical," "domestic," and "romantic"; Beth is "shy," "sweet," and "gentle"; and Amy is "artistic," "selfish," and "annoying." Then Mrs. Hawthorne hands out next month's assignment and we're done.

As the others head back downstairs to the party, I duck into my bedroom on the second floor and quickly pull on my old hockey jersey. "Laguna Lightning" is printed on the front, and my number—77—is on the back. We were the top-ranked under-twelve PeeWee girls' hockey team in Southern California last year, with a shot at this year's state championship. Here in Concord, I have a shot at nothing.

I pull a goalie mask I found at a thrift store over my scowling face, stuff my dead giveaway red hair up in a wool hat, and head downstairs.

The house is already starting to fill up. I wander out to the kitchen, where a group of parents are standing around talking and laughing with my mom. I listen for a while, then I drift into the family room, where kids from school are milling around drinking punch and soda and eating veggies and dip. My sister, who is dressed in her cheerleader's uniform, appears bearing platters of pizza, and everybody crowds around.

So far, just as I'd hoped, nobody recognizes me. I move through the crowd like a ghost. The Fab Four are huddled by the punch bowl (a big black plastic cauldron—where does my mother find this stuff?). They're all dressed as pop stars, just like Megan. They're supposed to be some group, I guess. I edge closer to hear what they're talking about.

"I'd give anything to have hair like that," says Megan, staring enviously at my sister's long blonde hair.

"But your hair is perfect!" Ashley protests. Megan makes a face, but I can tell she's pleased at the compliment. The Fab Four are always sucking up to one another. It's revolting.

"How did Cassidy ever get into this family?" says Jen. "She doesn't look a thing like her mother or sister."

"Maybe she's adopted," Megan suggests.

Heather Vogel Frederick

"Who'd adopt a creep like her?" asks Ashley.

"A witch?" Becca replies slyly. The four of them look over at my mother and laugh. I can feel my face growing hot under the hockey mask.

"Check out Emma Hawthorne," says Megan, nodding toward the sofa across the room. "What a baby. Her costume looks like something a kindergartner would wear."

"That's not a very nice thing to say about your little book club pal," Becca says with a smirk.

Megan flips her hair back angrily. "I told you, that stupid club wasn't my idea."

"My mom told my dad that Jess's parents are probably going to get a divorce," says Becca, her voice dropping to a whisper. Her friends lean closer. "My mom says her mom's never coming back from New York."

Megan looks over toward the couch, where Jess and Emma are sitting by themselves eating pizza. Emma has a big smear of tomato sauce on her chin. "Can you blame her?" she says. "Have you ever had to sit next to Goat Girl? P-U! Who'd want to come back to a kid like that. Get it? Kid? *Goat* Girl?"

There's a pause as the rest of the Fab Four process the pun. Finally, they burst into exaggerated laughter, like Megan said something incredibly witty.

I decide I can't take any more of this, and I walk over to my teammates. "Hey, guys."

They stare at me for a minute.

"Cassidy?" says Zach finally. He's wearing a box that's been spray-painted silver. He's supposed to be a robot.

I lift my goalie mask up a couple of inches, enough for him to see my face. "Yup, it's me. Cool costume. Are you guys up for tricks instead of treats tonight?"

Ethan, who is dressed as Count Dracula, lifts a dark eyebrow. "What kind of tricks?"

"Scaring the socks off those four," I reply with a nod toward the punch bowl.

"So what's your plan?" asks Third, his tall clown's hat bobbing as he glances skeptically at the Fab Four.

"I need you to get them to Sleepy Hollow Cemetery. I'll take care of the rest."

"Sleepy Hollow, huh? We're going to need some bait," says Zach.

"That would be you," I tell him.

He turns beet red.

"C'mon, Zach, you know Megan likes you! All you have to do is tell her you want to go with her for a walk. It'll be worth it, I promise."

"I guess," he says reluctantly.

"It's not like you have to, you know, kiss her or anything," I reassure him, and Ethan and Third instantly start making smoochy noises. "Just get her there, then leave the rest to me."

"Sounds like fun," says Third.

"For you, maybe," grumbles Zach.

"Meet me by Emerson's grave," I tell them. "You know, that huge

Heather Vogel Frederick

white rock on Author's Ridge. And whatever you do, don't tell them I'm there."

Ethan looks at me curiously. "How come you know so much about Sleepy Hollow? I thought you just moved here."

"I dunno," I mumble, suddenly embarrassed. "I've ridden my bike there a couple of times, that's all." Back in California I visited Dad's grave nearly every day, and the habit just stuck, I guess. Cemeteries aren't nearly as creepy as people think. At least not in the daytime. Riding around a graveyard is kind of like being at the rink. It's quiet, and the paths are smooth as ice. I can hear myself think there, the same way I can when I'm skating. Maybe that's weird. I don't know.

Across the room, Emma is staring at Zach like he's the last cupcake on the platter. I shake my head and slip into the kitchen to find a flashlight and some duct tape. I just don't get it. What is so special about Zach Norton? He's a nice guy and everything, but he's just, well, Zach.

The parents have all moved into the living room by now, and as Zach and Ethan and Third and the Fab Four head toward the front door, Mrs. Chadwick, who is dressed as a nurse, looks up. "Are you kids all going trick-or-treating?"

"Yes, Mom," Becca replies.

Emphasis on trick, I think, grinning to myself under the goalie mask.

Mrs. Chadwick looks triumphantly over at Mrs. Sloane and Mrs. Hawthorne. "Well, you and your *friends* have fun, okay? And be back here by nine. It's a school night."

The party starts to break up. Emma and Jess start to leave too, and it suddenly occurs to me that I could use some help. "Hey!" I call after them.

They turn and stare at me. "Cassidy? Is that you?" says Emma.

I push the mask up on top of my head so they can see my face. "Are you two up for some fun?"

They exchange a wary glance. "What kind of fun?" asks Emma.

I grab their arms and steer them down the hall in reply. My mother notices the three of us and her green witch face lights up. Now it's her turn to smile triumphantly at Mrs. Chadwick. "Have a great time, girls!" she calls.

Once past the parent-infested living room, I whisk the black cape off the vampire sitting at the head of our dining room table—*Dad's chair,* I can't help thinking—then fish my hockey stick out of the front hall closet. "Here, you carry these," I say, thrusting them at Emma and Jess. They take the cape and stick reluctantly.

"What are they for?" Emma asks.

"Ever heard of the Headless Horseman?"

She and Jess exchange another glance. "Sure," Emma replies. "But what does a hockey stick have to do with him?"

"You'll see." I close the front door behind us, look back over my shoulder to make sure nobody's watching from the window, then grab the battery-operated jack-o'-lantern from the bottom of our front steps. Emma and Jess trail reluctantly behind me as I head down Hubbard Street toward town.

Ahead under the streetlights, I spot my teammates with the Fab

Four. They turn left at the post office, heading for Main Street.

"We'll take the shortcut through the parking lot," I tell Emma and Jess, prodding them forward across Walden. "It's quicker."

"A shortcut to where?" asks Emma, who is already huffing and puffing. She really needs to take up a sport.

"You'll see," I say again.

"You keep saying that, but we don't see," she complains.

I sigh. "Sleepy Hollow."

Jess stops in her tracks. Emma, who is taking up the rear, nearly runs into her. "*The graveyard?*" squeaks Jess. "On Halloween?"

"You've got to be joking!" adds Emma.

"Don't be such babies," I snap. "Don't you want to give the Fab Four a taste of their own medicine?"

Jess looks nervous at this news. So does Emma. "We're not going to get in trouble, are we?" she asks.

I put my hands on my hips and glare at them scornfully. "You two are completely hopeless!" I tell them. "How do you ever manage to have any fun? Stop being such goody-goodies. We're not going to get in trouble. We're just going to spice up their Halloween a little."

"Well, okay, I guess," says Emma finally. Jess doesn't say anything, but she doesn't turn back, either.

"Come on then, we have to hurry." I can hear squeals and giggles from the Fab Four. They're only a few blocks behind us. I pick up the pace a little as we cross Monument Square, and soon Emma is huffing and puffing again.

I grab her by the elbow and pull her along. My flashlight's lone beam is nearly lost in the total darkness of the graveyard, but the three of us manage to stumble our way up Author's Ridge. When we reach Ralph Waldo Emerson's grave, I shove Emma and Jess behind it. We all flop down in the grass and lean back against the cold granite, panting.

"Give me the hockey stick," I say, and Emma hands it over. I tape the vampire cloak around the handle.

"Jack-o'-lantern," I order, holding out my hand like a surgeon asking for a scalpel on one of those TV shows. Jess hands it over and I loop the handle of the jack-o'-lantern over the blade of the stick and tape it down securely, too.

"Check it out!" I crow, hoisting my hockey stick in the air and waving it slowly back and forth. The cape billows out perfectly, and the movement activates the lantern's blinking red eyes and evil chuckle.

"You really think that's going to scare them?" Emma sounds dubious.

"It'll scare them all right, just you wait and see," I reply. "It's the last thing they'll be expecting. Now, can you two hold this up just like I did and wave it around when I give you the signal?"

They both nod.

"Good." We squat down quietly behind the tombstone and wait. It doesn't take long.

"Ooo, it's creepy in here, Zach," I hear Megan say. "Where are we going?"

Heather Vogel Frederick

"You're in that book club with Cassidy, right?" Zach replies. "I just thought you might like to see Louisa May Alcott's grave."

Third hoots like an owl, and the girls all shriek. The boys laugh. They come to a halt on the other side of the stone.

"That's not Louisa's grave, that's Emerson's," says Becca.

"It's showtime," I whisper to Emma and Jess, and, cupping my hands around my mouth, I call out "Megan!" in the deepest, weirdest, spookiest voice I can muster.

She gives a little squeal. "Who's there?" I can't see her, but I'd bet my championship hockey jersey that she's clutching Zach Norton's arm.

"The Headless Horseman!" I moan.

"There is no such thing," Megan replies, but she doesn't sound so sure.

"That's what you think!" I moan again. "The Headless Horseman is for real, Megan, and he's come for YOU!"

I give Emma and Jess the thumbs up. They hoist the hockey stick into the air, and slowly the black-cloaked figure rises above Ralph Waldo's grave. I motion to them again and they wave it back and forth. The movement triggers the motion detector, and the jack-o'-lantern's eyes blink open and begin to glow red. "Mwa-ha-ha-ha," it chuckles, the evil laugh gradually rising in pitch. "Mwa-ha-ha-ha-HA!"

I leap out from behind the tombstone, holding the flashlight under my chin and shining it on the white goalie mask that covers my face. The Fab Four's screams split the air, and this time there's real fear in their voices. I lunge at Megan and she drops Zach's arm and takes off running. Becca and Ashley and Jen are right behind her, hanging onto one another for dear life as they skid down the steep path. I chase them all the way to the cemetery entrance, then double back.

Zach and Ethan and Third are collapsed on the ground, howling.

"Cassidy, you rule!" gasps Third. "That was awesome!"

I nod smugly. For the first time since we moved to Concord, I feel really, truly happy. Dad would have loved this. I untape the jack-o'-lantern from my hockey stick. As I do so, it blinks again and chuckles.

The boys stagger to their feet. I shine my flashlight around, looking for Emma and Jess. The beam bounces off Emma's glasses and highlights Jess's wild white wig.

"Hey!" crows Ethan. "I didn't know that Hawthorne the Heifer and Goat Girl were here!"

"Shut up, MacDonald," says Zach. He reaches over and slaps Emma and Jess both a high five.

Even though it's pitch-black, I can tell that Emma is blushing. I smile. "Enough with the tricks," I say. "Let's go get some treats."

And as we head back to town, I can't resist doing a little victory dance. Final score: Cassidy-1; Fab Four-0.

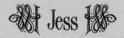 Jess

"November is the most disagreeable month in the whole year . . ."

"Why not, Jess? You'd be perfect for the part!"

The skating rink is cold, and I wrap my fleece jacket tighter around me. "Quit bugging me, Emma. The answer is no."

"I'll help you learn your lines," she coaxes, thrusting the script under my nose.

I shake my head. Emma sighs. "C'mon, Jess, you've got to at least think about it. You've got such a great voice!"

I stare out at the ice. Doesn't Emma get it? My mother ran away from home last summer to be an *actress*. The last thing I want to do is try out for the middle school musical.

"They should be starting soon," I say, trying to distract her. Emma is like a dog with a bone when she gets an idea in her head.

Emma turns to look at the cluster of skaters at the far end of the rink. Today is tryouts for the Concord Comets, the middle school boys' hockey team, and there are about a zillion hopefuls warming up, including Emma's brother Darcy, Darcy's best friend Kyle Anderson, and Third.

"Well, if it isn't the little women."

We turn around to see Becca and Ashley and Jen sliding into the seats behind us. Becca eyes Emma's winter jacket. "Another Nicole Patterson original?"

Emma reddens.

I scowl at Becca and her wannabees. I hate it when they pick on Emma. She can't help it if her family's on a tight budget.

The three of them just laugh. Emma and I turn our attention back to the rink and try and ignore them.

Out on the ice, the coach blows his whistle and divides the boys into four groups.

"He's going to put them through some drills," Emma explains. I've been to a few games, but I don't know anything about hockey. Emma's been watching her brother skate since she was still drinking out of a sippy cup.

The coach blows his whistle again. The first group of skaters takes off down the ice.

"Full speed!" the coach shouts. "Keep your heads up and stop at the blue line!"

After all the skaters reach the line, the coach blows his whistle again and they sprint toward the next one.

"Bend your knees!" hollers the coach, and so it continues on down the ice, group after group.

I search the crowd for a skater in a blue-and-white jersey.

"There," whispers Emma, nudging me with her elbow. "With Third, in this next group."

Heather Vogel Frederick

Behind us, Becca and Ashley and Jen are cheering for Becca's older brother, Stewart. We keep our eyes on the blue-and-white jersey, though, which streaks down the ice at the head of the pack, making each blue-line stop crisply and cleanly.

Next, the coach sets up orange cones down the middle of the rink.

"Glide turns," says Emma, and we watch as one by one the skaters swoop down the rink, carving their way in and out of the cones.

"Two hands on the stick!" the coach yells, startling Stewart Chadwick, who stumbles and trips over a cone and drops his stick completely.

"How's your brother doing?" a voice behind us booms.

It's Becca's mother. She's carrying a tray from the concession stand loaded with sodas and a jumbo popcorn. Megan Wong is with her.

"Fabulous, Mom," Becca replies.

"Actually, he's terrible," Emma whispers to me, and we both giggle.

Mrs. Chadwick maneuvers her massive behind into a seat and glares at us. "You two troublemakers again. I've got my eye on you."

Ever since Halloween, Mrs. Chadwick has been on the warpath. The Fab Four were practically in hysterics by the time they got back to the Sloanes' house from Sleepy Hollow, and, unfortunately, Cassidy's white hockey mask was a dead giveaway and she got caught. Mrs. Sloane grounded her for a month for pulling the prank. Cassidy didn't rat Emma and me out, and we certainly didn't offer any information, but still, Mrs. Chadwick is suspicious.

After glide turns the skaters are paired up, two playing offense and two playing defense. At the whistle the offensive players race for the net, trying to get past the defense and score. Darcy and Kyle easily dodge Stewart Chadwick and some other player I don't recognize, whipping the puck back and forth between them until Darcy takes a shot and scores.

"Walk in the park," says Emma. She stands up and shouts, "Way to go, Darcy!"

"You're blocking my view!" snaps Mrs. Chadwick.

Looking flustered, Emma sits down. But it's not Becca's mother who's got her rattled. A few rows ahead of us, Zach Norton and Ethan MacDonald slide into a pair of seats to watch.

The whistle blows again and the blue-and-white jersey streaks down the ice, skips nimbly past the line of defense, zips toward the goal, and scores.

The coach makes a mark on his checkboard. "You! Number 77! Over there!" he yells, pointing to the skaters clustered to the left of the goal. I spot Darcy, Kyle, and Third amongst them. Stewart Chadwick is grouped with the players on the right.

Emma leans in close and whispers in my ear, "She just made the first cut."

The skater in the blue-and-white jersey is Cassidy Sloane. Not that anyone could tell just by looking. With their helmets and mouth guards and everything, everyone looks alike.

"Do you think Zach will guess?" Emma asks.

I give her a sidelong glance. Emma's voice goes all soft and mushy when she says Zach's name, and her face gets red whenever he's

Heather Vogel Frederick

around. Just like it is now. Emma thinks she's got everybody fooled, but I know she likes Zach Norton.

I've never told anyone who I like. Not even my mom, and I tell her everything. Or I used to, before she ran away from home. That's what we call it, my dad and me. He says she'll be back, that she's just trying to figure life out, but I'm not so sure. I try not to think about the *D* word, but I can't help it. That's *D* as in *Divorce*, of course.

I watch Cassidy swoop down the ice again as the coach puts the players through more drills, and I remind myself that things could be worse. It could be *D* as in *Death* instead. Cassidy never mentions her dad, but Emma and I overheard Emma's parents talking about him last spring when the Sloanes first moved to town. "A tragic car accident," they called it.

"Emma, your brother was team captain last year, right?" Mrs. Chadwick demands suddenly.

Emma jumps, then nods in response.

"Why isn't my son standing with him and those other boys?"

I lean in close to Emma. "Maybe because he stinks at hockey," I whisper.

Emma kicks me, trying not to laugh. "Um, I'm not sure," she replies.

Becca's mother looks at us, her eyes narrowing in suspicion. "I'm going to talk to the coach," she informs the Fab Four. "Don't eat all the popcorn." And with that she lumbers off, her face a thundercloud.

"Do you really think this is going to work?" I whisper to Emma.

"I don't see why not," Emma whispers back. "Darcy's right—Cassidy's good. Really good. She'll definitely make the team, but I don't know whether she'll get to stay once Coach Danner finds out. He's kind of old-fashioned."

One glance at his crew cut had already told me that. "Maybe he won't find out," I say hopefully.

"Whisper, whisper, whisper," mocks Megan. "You two are full of secrets today, aren't you?"

We're whispering because nobody knows Cassidy is trying out except me, Emma, and Darcy. Technically, Cassidy is still grounded, but we felt we owed it to her when she asked us to help. We figured it was the least we could do, since she covered for us on Halloween.

"All you have to do is invite me over after school before the next book club meeting," Cassidy told us. "I'll tell my mother that you're going to help tutor me in science"—Cassidy got a D on the last test—"and that we're going to bake cookies for the book club meeting. I'm sure she'll let me come."

It sounded simple enough, and we said okay because it wasn't really a lie. Cassidy really did come home on the bus with us this afternoon to Emma's house. And I really did help her with her science homework. She only stayed for a little while, though, before she got her bike and the hockey stuff she'd had Emma come by and get the day before, and took off for the rink. At the last minute, we had to let Darcy in on the secret, too, because Cassidy panicked when she realized she'd forgotten her helmet.

"I can't go home to get it!" she'd wailed. "My mother is there!"

Heather Vogel Frederick

"Can't go home to get what?" Darcy had said, walking in on the commotion. "Never mind, I think I know," he'd added, as soon as he spotted Cassidy's hockey uniform.

We ended up telling him, and he was really cool about the whole thing, which he always is. Emma's lucky to have such a nice brother. Darcy promised not to tell, and said Cassidy was one of the best skaters he'd ever seen and he wouldn't mind having her on the team even if she was a girl. He even found an old helmet for her to wear, and he gave her some advice, to boot.

"You've got to show Coach Danner what you've got right out of the starting gate," he told her. "Don't hold anything back. He doesn't give second chances."

From the looks of it, Cassidy took Darcy's advice, because now she's standing with all the skaters who made the first cut. She glances over at us and Emma and I give her a thumbs-up. She waves her stick in response.

"I know a secret too," says Becca Chadwick.

We turn around. All the color drains out of Emma's face. Becca is holding her journal, the new one she got for book club. She must have taken it out of Emma's backpack while we were watching Cassidy.

"Oh, Za-ach!" Becca calls. "I've got something you need to hear!"

"Give me that!" shrieks Emma, leaping up from her seat and snatching at the journal. Becca waves it over her head, just out of reach.

"Defense!" orders Becca, and Megan and Ashley and Jen obediently close ranks between her and Emma.

Zach and Ethan come up to see what all the commotion is about.

"Becca, don't," Emma pleads. Her mouth is trembling and there are tears in her eyes. "Give it back!"

Becca waves it again, taunting. "Who's going to make me? Goat Girl?"

"What's going on?" says Zach.

"Emma wrote a poem for you," Becca informs him snarkily.

Stricken, Emma turns and stares beseechingly at Megan. "Please, Megan, make her stop," she begs.

A flash of sympathy flickers across Megan's face. "Maybe this isn't such a hot idea, Becca," she says.

"Oh, that's right," says Becca coldly. "I forgot. You two are buddies again now that you're in that precious book club."

Megan and Becca lock eyes. After a moment, Megan looks away. Becca opens the journal with a triumphant flourish. "'Zach Attack,' by Emma Hawthorne," she announces, and Ashley and Jen start to snicker. So does Ethan. Megan looks uncomfortable, but she doesn't say a word. Zach looks like he doesn't know what to think. Emma looks like she's going to faint. Becca starts to read.

"Hair like summer sunshine.
Eyes the color of the wind.
A smile that makes my heart stop.
Whenever he comes in."

"Oh, man," mumbles Zach, his face flaming, "I don't think I can listen to this." He clamps his hands over his ears and stumbles back toward his seat.

Ethan hoots with laughter. "Zach has a secret admirer—Hawthorne the Heifer!"

"Wait!" shrieks Becca. "You didn't hear the best part!" She yells out the rest of the verse. "'My heart stops! Flip flops! Zach is back! Zach is back! And I'm having another Zach attack!'"

The Fab Four howl, taking up the refrain. "I'm having another Zach attack!"

"That's enough," says a cool voice.

The Fab Four start guiltily. Mrs. Hawthorne is standing beside them. Ethan melts away. Mrs. Hawthorne holds out her hand. Without a word, Becca hands the journal to her. Mrs. Hawthorne gives her a reproachful look. "You know better, Rebecca Chadwick." She turns to Megan. "And I'm surprised at you, too, Megan."

Megan looks at the floor.

Sobbing, Emma hurls herself at her mother. Mrs. Hawthorne puts her arms around her. "Did I see your mother here, Becca?"

Becca nods.

"Go get her for me, would you, please? I need to have a word with her."

The Fab Four vanish, leaving me and Emma alone with her mother. Mrs. Hawthorne slips the journal into her daughter's backpack.

"Why don't you wait for me in the car, honey," she says, pulling a tissue out of her purse and dabbing at Emma's eyes and tear-stained glasses. "Tryouts will be over soon and then we can go home."

"I can't believe they'd do that!" Emma wails.

"I know, honey," says her mother, her voice gentle. "It was cruel and heartless and you didn't deserve it."

"I've never been so humiliated in my entire life," Emma sniffles. "I want to go home right now."

"I have to wait for Darcy," her mother says.

"We brought our bikes," I tell Mrs. Hawthorne. "Maybe we could just ride home."

Mrs. Hawthorne nods, and Emma runs out of the rink.

She's already on her bike and pedaling like fury by the time I get to mine. I don't catch up with her until we reach the library. Emma zips across Main Street and heads for the shortcut to Lowell Road, just past Colonial Academy. I follow, burrowing my chin in my jacket against the sharp November wind.

"I hate Becca Chadwick's guts!" Emma shouts, the wind whipping her words back to me. "Ethan's, too! And I'll never forgive Megan as long as I live!"

She skids to a stop in front of her house, abandons her bike on the lawn, and dashes into the house. I'm right behind her.

"Hey, girls!" Mr. Hawthorne calls as he hears us come in. He pokes his head out of his study. Emma rushes past and pelts up the stairs to her room.

"Everything okay?" asks her father, frowning.

Heather Vogel Frederick

"Um, not exactly," I tell him, explaining what happened.

He goes upstairs after Emma. I head to the kitchen. The clock on the wall ticks softly as I rummage for butter and eggs and all the other ingredients we need for making cookies. Then I settle in at the kitchen table with my homework.

I love the Hawthornes' kitchen. Emma's mother painted it pink, and it's always cheerful, even on a cold gray afternoon like this one. There are a handful of places on earth where I feel completely safe, and the Hawthornes' kitchen is one of them. Our barn at home is another.

Melville, the Hawthornes' orange tiger cat, comes in to see what we're up to. He twines himself around my legs, then hops up into my lap.

"Hey, Mel," I say softly, scratching him under the chin. "How's it going?"

Mel sniffs my jeans cautiously. He probably smells Sugar, and maybe our horses and goats, too. I overslept this morning and didn't have time to change after chores. I tickle him with the end of my braid and he swats at it playfully, then starts to knead my leg, purring as he snuggles down for a nap.

Melville likes me. Most animals do. In fact, I've been thinking that maybe I'd like to be a veterinarian when I grow up. Animals are a lot less complicated than people. Especially dogs. Dogs love you, and that's that. They don't betray their friends, and they'd never do something low-down like reading your journal aloud in public. Dogs never leave the people they love. Dogs don't run off to New York to be actors.

Emma finally reappears. Her eyes are still red, but she's washed her face and is looking calmer.

"Did you finish the assignment for book club?" she asks me.

"Yeah."

"I didn't quite finish chapter 10. I've read it before, but it was ages ago and I can't remember what happens. Do you think you could read it out loud while I start the cookies?"

"Sure," I reply. I nudge Melville gently off my lap and pull *Little Women* out of my backpack. Across the kitchen, Emma starts to measure and sift and pour.

"Which March sister do you like best?" she asks me as I flip through the pages.

"Jo, of course," I reply.

"Me, too," says Emma. She cracks one egg into the dough, then another. Emma is a really good cook, just like her dad. And just like him, she's a good writer, too. That "Zach Attack" poem was pretty good. I loved the line, "Eyes the color of the wind." Not that I'd ever bring it up.

Emma measures out a teaspoon of vanilla, then another. This is her secret ingredient for chocolate chip cookies—an extra teaspoon of vanilla. I know this because we make chocolate chip cookies at her house at least once a week.

"Which sister do you think you're most like?" she asks me, popping a handful of chocolate chips into her mouth.

I shrug. "Beth, maybe."

Heather Vogel Frederick

Emma cocks her head and studies me. "Definitely Beth," she says. "You love animals and music, and you're, you know—shy."

I give her a wry smile. "I wish I was more like Jo. She's not afraid of anything."

"I know. I wish I was more like her too. Jo wouldn't let Becca Chadwick walk all over her."

"But you are like Jo! You want to be a writer, don't you?"

Emma dumps the rest of the chocolate chips into the cookie dough. "Yeah, but I think I'm more like Meg in some ways. I'm not as brave as Jo, and I'm kind of a homebody."

I find chapter 10. "'As spring came on, a new set of amusements became the fashion,'" I begin, and quickly find myself wrapped up in the antics of the Pickwick Club. I haven't said a word to anyone, not even Emma, but I really like *Little Women.* Reading about the March family gives me that same safe feeling as being in my barn and in the Hawthornes' pink kitchen.

Emma smiles when I get to the part about Laurie setting up a post office in an old birdhouse where he and the March girls can leave one another presents and letters.

"'The P.O. was a capital little institution, and flourished wonderfully,'" I read, as Emma slides the sheet of cookies into the oven. She passes me a spoonful of dough. I take a nibble, then read on, describing the various surprises the friends leave in the birdhouse. Emma licks her spoon thoughtfully as I read about the gardener who sends a love letter to Hannah, the Marches' decidedly unromantic housekeeper. "'How they laughed when the secret came out, never dreaming how many love letters that little post office would hold in the years to come!'"

"Do you think we'll ever get love letters?" Emma asks. She has a faraway look on her face, and I figure she's thinking about Zach.

I hesitate. I can't imagine anybody wanting to write me one, that's for sure. And Emma? I look at the flour streaked across her round, cheerful face and the smear of chocolate on the front of her shirt. Emma is my best friend in the whole world, but to be honest I can't imagine anybody writing a love letter to her, either. Especially not Zach Norton. But I don't tell her that.

"Sure," I tell her. "We'll get dozens of love letters someday."

"I remember the first time I read *Little Women*," Emma continues. "I couldn't wait to find out who would write love letters to Jo!"

I laugh. "And remember how I'd seen the movie and knew what happened?" I recall. "I tried to tell you, but you covered your ears with your hands and screamed."

"Did I really scream?"

"Oh, yeah. You wouldn't let me tell you."

"Nope," says Emma, shaking her head. "I remember that part. I didn't want you to spoil it for me. I wanted to read the book and find out for myself."

I look down at the book, and think about the heartbreak that I know is waiting for the March family and their friends. Just like real life, not all stories end happily. Sometimes friends betray us, and the people we love don't always love us back. Sometimes people die or leave us. I don't know yet if there will be a happy ending for me and my family. If life were a book, would I want to skip ahead to the ending? Or would I rather wait and read along to find out, like Emma said? I'm not sure. I close *Little Women* and set it on the table.

The buzzer goes off and Mr. Hawthorne appears in the doorway, sniffing hopefully. "Is that chocolate chip cookies I smell?"

"Perfect timing," says Emma, taking the tray out of the oven.

Mr. Hawthorne settles in across the table from me. "*Little Women*, eh?" he says, picking it up. "A great American classic. I'm more of a Huck Finn kind of guy myself, but I guess it's a girl thing. I know your mother is having a wonderful time with this book club, Emma. You girls enjoying it too?"

"Sort of," says Emma, and I nod.

"That's good. I know it means a lot to your mother, Emma, to be able to spend some time with you." Mr. Hawthorne pauses and looks over at me, his brown eyes thoughtful. Both of us are suddenly aware that there is a big hole in the conversation. Normally he would have said, "And to your mother too, Jess," but of course he can't because she's not here. After a minute he continues lightly, "I saw your brothers the other day at the grocery store, Jess. They sure are growing up fast. Are they in kindergarten this year?"

"First grade."

"Holy mackerel! Already?" Mr. Hawthorne shakes his head. "It seems like just last year you girls were in first grade." He holds his hand out for a cookie. Emma passes him one and he takes a bite.

"Mmmmm. Perfect. How about Half Moon Farm? Things going well? How's your father doing?"

I feel my face grow hot. How does he think my father is doing, for Pete's sake? I can only imagine how Mr. Hawthorne would be be doing if Mrs. Hawthorne had left and the whole town knew it because her face was plastered all over the TV every afternoon at three thirty. But Mr. Hawthorne isn't trying to be mean, he's just being polite, so I don't say any of that. "Okay, I guess," I mumble instead.

Mr. Hawthorne reaches across the table and pats my hand gently. He pushes back from the table. "There's a casserole in the fridge, girls. Would you mind popping it in when you're done with your baking?" He grabs another cookie as he heads for the door. "I'll be in my study if you need anything."

When the cookies are finished, Emma puts the casserole in the oven and we get started on our homework. I'm helping Emma with math when we hear the front door open.

"It's them!" Emma jumps up and runs out of the kitchen. I'm right behind her.

"I can't believe the nerve of that man," Mrs. Hawthorne takes off her coat and gives it an angry shake. "And that woman. Shame on them both."

"Shame on who both?" asks Mr. Hawthorne, poking his head out of his study again. "What's going on? Didn't you make the team, Darcy?"

Heather Vogel Frederick

"Oh, I made it," says Darcy. He grins. "So did Cassidy."

Emma whoops and we both rush over to congratulate her. Cassidy slaps us each a high five.

Emma's father's eyebrows nearly spring off his forehead. "Cassidy made the *boys'* team?"

"That's the point, dear," says Mrs. Hawthorne crisply. "There is no girls' team at the middle school. And until he found out Cassidy was a girl, Coach Danner was all set to let her play."

"You should see her skate, Dad!" says Darcy. "She's awesome!"

"Is that right?" Mr. Hawthorne replies, giving Cassidy a bemused look.

"It's a good thing I arrived when I did to pick up Darcy," Mrs. Hawthorne continues, pulling a hanger out of the hall closet and jabbing it into the sleeves of her coat. "When I heard what had happened, I reminded Coach Danner in no uncertain terms about Title IX. By federal law, he cannot discriminate on the basis of gender. Cassidy is entitled to a spot on that team."

"I'll bet Bob was delighted to hear that," says Emma's father under his breath.

Mrs. Hawthorne shoots him a look. "The law is the law."

"So how come he didn't know Cassidy was a girl?"

Cassidy holds up Darcy's old helmet.

"Aha," says Mr. Hawthorne. "Of course." He looks at Emma and me. "Do I detect a small conspiracy here? A pair of partners in crime? Wasn't Cassidy supposed to spend the afternoon here, doing homework with you two?"

I am suddenly fascinated by the pattern in the hall carpet. Emma is staring down at it too.

"'Oh! What a tangled web we weave,'" Emma's father continues solemnly. "Sir Walter Scott. However, to be fair—and to quote yet another literary immortal, Shakespeare this time—'all's well that ends well.'"

"And that Calliope Chadwick!" continues Mrs. Hawthorne.

"What did the harpy do this time?"

"Her son Stewart didn't make the team, and she's got it in her head that somehow it's all Cassidy's fault, that if she would just resign gracefully, Stewart would be put on the team in her place."

Mr. Hawthorne's forehead puckers. "Is that true?"

Darcy shakes his head. "No way, Dad. Stewart can barely skate."

"And then to top it off, that blister of a daughter of hers stole Emma's journal out of her backpack and read part of it aloud to some boys."

"So I hear," Mr. Hawthorne says soberly.

"WHAT?!" Cassidy explodes. "Becca Chadwick is a weasel!"

"Now, Cassidy," says Mrs. Hawthorne.

"But she is!"

Mrs. Hawthorne sighs. "Well, yes, in this case I would say she certainly exhibited weasel-like behavior. I had a word with her mother about that."

"Uh-oh," says Mr. Hawthorne. "And how did Mama Bear feel about having her cub criticized?"

Heather Vogel Frederick

"Let's just say it didn't go over very well," Emma's mother replies.

The buzzer on the oven goes off again.

"Dinner is served," announces Mr. Hawthorne.

Emma and I set the table while Cassidy and Darcy quickly shower and change. The dining room is my next-favorite room at the Hawthornes' house, after the kitchen. There are shelves on all four walls, and they're lined with books. I've never seen a dining room with books in it before. In fact, I've never seen a house with so many books in it, period. My house has books too, but not nearly so many. We have more animals, though, and sometimes they wind up in the house, even the ones that shouldn't. Mom used to hate that.

The only animal the Hawthornes have is Melville, who has followed us into the dining room in hopes of snagging himself a front-row seat at the coming meal. I give him a quick pat as Mr. Hawthorne sets garlic bread and salad on the table with the macaroni and cheese. Everything smells delicious.

"I'm starved," says Darcy.

"Me, too," echoes Cassidy, and as we dig in the two of them give us a hilarious blow-by-blow of Stewart Chadwick's bungled hockey tryout.

"Speaking of tryouts," says Emma finally, "I have an announcement to make."

We all look over at her.

"Jess is going to try out for the lead in *Beauty and the Beast*."

My fork stops halfway between my plate and my mouth. "Emma!" I protest, mortified. "I told you—the answer is no."

"The middle school musical? Perfect!" says Mrs. Hawthorne enthusiastically. "With your voice, you'd make a wonderful Belle."

"She's right, Jess," says Darcy. "I remember hearing you at Emma's chorus concert last spring. That solo you sang? It was really good."

"Really?" The word comes out a squeak, and I blush.

He reaches over and tugs on my braid. His brown eyes are warm. "Sure."

"See, Jess?" says Emma smugly. "I told you."

I stare down at my macaroni and cheese like I'm looking at it through a microscope. I've never noticed before how much elbow noodles look like amoebas. I prod at them with my fork. "Maybe," I say finally.

Before anybody can say anything else, there's a knock at the door. Mrs. Hawthorne glances at her watch. "The book club!" she exclaims. "I almost forgot."

"Darcy and I will do the dishes," says Mr. Hawthorne. "You ladies go join your guests."

"I hope we're not too early," says Mrs. Wong, as Mrs. Hawthorne opens the front door.

"Don't be silly," Mrs. Hawthorne replies. "Friends can never be too early. Come on in, we're just finishing up."

Megan looks a little surprised to see me and Cassidy sitting at the dinner table. For a second, I catch a flash of another emotion on her face. Disappointment, maybe, but the expression is fleeting. She coolly pulls her cell phone from her purse and taps out a text message while Emma's mother hangs up their coats.

Heather Vogel Frederick

We're all moving into the living room when there's another knock at the door. It's Clementine Sloane, and she doesn't even say hello, she just strides in. She does not look happy.

"Did you put her up to this?" she demands, glaring at Emma's mother.

"Put who up to what?" Mrs. Hawthorne blinks at her, confused.

"Cassidy went behind my back and tried out for the boys' hockey team," Mrs. Sloane explains grimly. "No sooner do I get off the phone with Calliope Chadwick, who has her knickers in a twist because Cassidy took her son's place on the team—or so she tells me—than I get a call from Coach Danner. He said something about Title IX, and that he'd checked and the town librarian was right, that legally Cassidy is entitled to a spot on the team."

Mrs. Hawthorne looks over at me and Emma and Cassidy, then back at Mrs. Sloane. "I see," she says slowly. "Clementine, please believe me, I had no idea that Cassidy was at the rink without your permission."

Mrs. Sloane puts her hands on her hips. "She told me she'd been invited here after school," she snaps. "You mean to tell me you had no idea about that, either?"

"Of course I knew about that," says Mrs. Hawthorne. "The girls asked if they could spend the afternoon here before book club. They wanted to do their science homework together and make cookies for our meeting."

That fleeting expression I spotted earlier reappears on Megan's face when she hears this. But it disappears just as quickly.

"They were cooking something up all right, but it wasn't treats for the book club," retorts Mrs. Sloane.

"But, Mom, I made the team!" Cassidy protests. "The coach said I was one of the best skaters he'd ever seen—before he knew I was a girl, I mean."

"How did you keep it a secret?"

"The coach couldn't tell under the helmet."

"Your helmet's at home, on the hall bench," says Mrs. Sloane.

Cassidy's eyes slide over to the doorway, where Emma's brother and father are watching. Darcy starts to do a slow fade. "Um, I borrowed a helmet," she says.

"Borrowed? From whom? From Emma?"

Mr. Hawthorne steps into the room. "From my son, actually," he says, gripping Darcy firmly by the shoulder and drawing him forward.

"The whole family was in on this?" says Mrs. Sloane, her voice rising.

"Clementine, I told you, Nick and I had no idea that Cassidy went behind your back to do this," Mrs. Hawthorne says hastily. "As for the kids, well, all I can say is, it won't happen again."

"You're right about that," snaps Mrs. Sloane. "Cassidy, get your things."

"Now, Clementine, please—"

Across from Emma and me, Megan is looking like the cat who ate the canary. She's clearly loving the fact that we're in trouble and she's not.

"Excuse me, but did you say something about Title IX?" asks Mrs. Wong.

Heather Vogel Frederick

Megan's smug smile fades a little. Cassidy's mother nods.

"But that's fantastic!" Mrs. Wong exclaims. "This could be a ground-breaking event! Just think of the ripple effect it could have at schools across the state. We'll have to call the sports editor at the Boston *Post*. I can see the headlines: 'Cassidy Sloane: Concord's Rebel on Skates.'"

Mrs. Sloane narrows her gorgeous blue supermodel eyes. "Lily," she warns, "stay out of this. My daughter doesn't need to become the poster child for another one of your causes."

Megan's mother looks like she's been slapped. Megan looks embarrassed.

"But that's beside the point," Mrs. Sloane continues. "The point is that nobody should be interfering with my family. Nobody should be going behind my back, aiding and abetting my daughter in flouting my rules."

"You're right, Clementine, of course, and I apologize if that's what this looks like," says Mrs. Hawthorne. "Again, I assure you we never would have done any of this if we had known that you didn't approve." She hesitates for a moment, giving Cassidy a sidelong glance. Then she continues. "I understand how upset you are, but what's done is done. And from what I hear, Cassidy certainly proved herself out there on the ice today. Would it be such a terrible thing for her to play hockey?"

"Hockey is dangerous!" cries Mrs. Sloane. "Cassidy could get hurt! You know that as well as I do, Phoebe."

"Mom, I've been playing for years," Cassidy protests. "Dad never worried about me getting hurt."

The room falls silent at the mention of Cassidy's father.

Mrs. Hawthorne lays her hand gently on Clementine Sloane's arm. "Perhaps we could all sit down and discuss this calmly over cookies?"

"There's nothing to discuss," says Mrs. Sloane coldly, pulling away. "Cassidy, get your things."

"I wish you weren't my mother!" cries Cassidy, a mutinous look on her face. "I hate you!"

Now Mrs. Sloane is the one who looks like she's been slapped. Wordlessly, she grips Cassidy by the arm, gathers up her backpack and hockey bag, and marches her out of the room. She pauses by the front door and turns, giving us all one last glance. "I thought you were my friends," she says bitterly, and slams the door behind her.

Nobody says anything for a long minute. Then Mrs. Hawthorne sighs. "Well, girls, I guess book club is over for tonight."

"For tonight?" Emma whispers to me, as Megan and Mrs. Wong get their coats. "How about forever?"

She's probably right. I can't imagine Mrs. Sloane speaking to any of us again. Not after tonight. The club will probably be disbanded. I'm surprised to find that this makes me sad. I guess I like book club more than I thought I did.

Melville slinks out from under the sofa, where he's been hiding from all the loud voices. He hops up into my lap again, stretches, and starts to purr. I scratch him under his chin and bury my nose in his fur. At least Mel isn't angry.

Like I said, animals are a lot less complicated than people.

Heather Vogel Frederick

WINTER

"*What a trying world it is! No sooner do we get out of one trouble than down comes another.*"

—Little Women

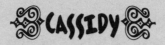

CASSIDY

*"Don't worry about me; I'll be as prim as I can,
and not get into any scrapes if I can help it."*

"Tell them to hurry," my mother says as we pull up in front of Walden Middle School. "Book club starts in half an hour."

"Okay." I hop out of our minivan and jog to the front door. Inside, the lobby is deserted. School always feels a little weird at night—all those empty, echoing hallways and closed lockers and dark classrooms.

I can hear faint strains of music from the auditorium, and I jog on down the hall, hoping I don't smell too bad. I've just come from hockey practice and haven't had a chance to shower yet.

After the disaster with the tryouts last month, my mother hauled me off to a shrink. Excuse me, "family counselor." But Dr. Weisman is really a shrink—I saw the diplomas on his wall. We sat there in his office and right in front of me my mother told him that she thought there was something seriously wrong with me, that ever since Dad died I'd been rebellious and sneaky and mean to her and that she couldn't handle my snotty attitude anymore. Then she burst into tears.

Dr. Weisman handed her a box of tissues. He sent me out into the waiting room so he could talk to her alone. After a while my mother came out and it was my turn. I thought maybe he was going to yell at me but the two of us just talked. He's pretty nice, for a shrink. He didn't ask about my dad, which was a good thing because I wasn't going to tell him anything anyway. We talked about hockey mostly. Turns out, he's a Bruins fan.

Dr. Weisman told me that my father's accident had shaken my mother up really badly, and that it had also made her hypersensitive to danger. He explained that right now what my mother most wanted was to keep her family safe, and that's why she sees hockey as a threat. He asked me if that made sense. I glared at him. So much for nice. I could see where this was going. He'd just been trying to butter me up with all his talk about the Bruins. He'd been on my mother's side all along.

"No more hockey forever, right?" I'd snapped.

Dr. Weisman had just smiled and asked me to go get my mother. I did and we all sat down again.

"Dr. Weisman thinks I should let you play hockey," my mother said stiffly.

I gaped at her, shocked. That was the absolute last thing I'd expected her to say. Then I catapulted out of my chair and punched my fist in the air. "Yes!" I crowed.

"Sit down, Cassidy," said Dr. Weisman. "Let your mother finish."

My mom looked down at her lap and twisted her tissue. "Dr. Weisman says that life is full of things that we can't control."

Well, duh, I could have told her that. She could have saved herself a lot of money. Shrinks are expensive.

"He says that while it's normal that I want to keep you safe, I need to be careful not to overdo it," she continued. "He said we've had so much sadness in our lives this past year that I need to think about what might make you happy. That I need to think about what's best for you, too, and not just what's best for me."

Dr. Weisman asked me if I knew what a compromise was. I said yeah, it's when people agree to give up stuff and do stuff to make other people happy. He said that's right, and explained that being able to compromise is especially important for families. He asked if I'd be willing to do a few things for my mother in exchange for being able to play hockey.

Was he kidding? I'd do *anything* to be able to play hockey!

As it turned out, my mother's conditions weren't too bad. I'm supposed to work on my attitude, mostly. She wants me to be more polite and respectful and not mouth off to her all the time. She wants me to be more ladylike and have better manners. I wasn't sure about the ladylike part, but I said I'd try.

Dr. Weisman had my mother and me sign a contract, and we're supposed to go see him once a month for a while. Just to talk about things.

So that's why I'm running down the hall at Walden Middle School wearing a Concord Comets uniform and smelling like a laundry hamper.

I open the door to the auditorium and slip into the back. Jessica Delaney is up on stage with Zach Norton. You could have knocked me over with a feather when I found out Zach had tried out for the play. Somehow I never took him for the actor type. He got one of the leads, too—he's playing Beast. I slip into the back row of seats and listen for a minute as he and Jess practice a duet. Emma was right: Jess has a great voice. Zach's not bad either.

"I still can't believe Goat Girl took your part!" I hear somebody whisper. I squint in the darkness and spot Becca Chadwick and the rest of the Fab Four sitting a few rows ahead of me.

Megan nods.

"Well, she only got it because her mother left and Mrs. Adams feels sorry for her," says Becca.

The other three heads bob in unison. The Fab Four all tried out for the play too, but they only got cast as dishes. Megan's a dancing plate, Becca's a cup, and Ashley and Jen are silverware. None of them are happy about this—especially Megan. She wanted to be Belle, and she and Becca have been busy spreading rumors ever since about why Jess got the part instead of her.

"Okay, cast, listen up!" says Mrs. Adams, the drama teacher, clapping her hands to get everyone's attention. "I want all lines for scenes one through six memorized by practice on Friday! We've only got two weeks until winter break, and we'll need to hit the ground running

Heather Vogel Frederick

when we come back in January if this show is going to be ready!"

Jess and Zach hop off the stage. I head down the aisle to meet them. "Jess, we've got to hurry," I tell her. "My mom's waiting in the parking lot."

"P-U, Sloane, you stink!" says Zach with a grin, waving his hand in front of his nose.

I grin back and punch him in the arm. "You think you're telling me something I don't know?"

"How's hockey going?" he asks. "You guys had your first game yet?"

I shake my head. "Nope. Saturday's the big day. You should come. We're going to wipe the rink with the Vikings."

"You think I'd miss a chance to see you and Third fall on your butts?"

I punch him in the arm again and we both laugh.

Behind me, I hear giggles. The Fab Four, of course. Like flies to honey—Zach being the honey.

"You have an awesome voice, Zach," coos Megan.

"Uh, thanks," says Zach, drifting away. He's kept his distance from the Fab Four ever since the whole "Zach Attack" thing. And he avoids Emma like the plague.

"We have to go," I tell Megan. "My mom's in the car waiting."

Becca looks me up and down. She wrinkles her nose. "Lucky you, Megan," she says sarcastically. "Goat Girl AND the Stinkbomb. Wish I was in your book club."

In response, I grab her in a bear hug and mash her face against my sweaty hockey jersey. "Who's a stinkbomb now?" I demand as she struggles and squeals. After a minute, I let her go, laughing. Insults rarely bother me, especially when they come from a lamebrain like Becca Chadwick. But I can see that it bothers Jess. She hates it when people call her "Goat Girl." Too bad she doesn't stick up for herself more.

"Dumb jock," Becca snaps, wiping her face with the sleeve of her sweater. "Nice friends, Megan."

"I told you, they're not my friends," says Megan coolly.

The three of us trudge out to the car in silence. Jess and I climb in the back, leaving Megan to sit up front with my mother.

"Hello, girls! How was play practice?" Without waiting for an answer, she turns around and sniffs loudly, like a bloodhound catching a whiff of steak. "Whew," she says. "Wish we had time to pop you in the shower. Do you have an extra shirt in your hockey bag?"

"Just the one I wore to school today."

"Well, go ahead and put it on. You're pretty ripe."

I'm on the brink of saying something snarky when I remember Dr. Weisman's contract. "Sure thing, Mom," I reply politely, and she smiles at me in the rearview mirror. As we pull out of the parking lot and head toward town, I crouch low in my seat and remove my smelly hockey jersey.

My mother makes a quick detour to Burger Barn, relaying our orders at the drive-thru window. As she pulls back onto the road, the only sound in the car is the hungry munching of burgers and fries.

Heather Vogel Frederick

"You three are awfully quiet tonight," says my mother finally.

I take a sip of soda and give Megan a sidelong glance. I can't resist. "You should hear Jess, Mom, she can really sing," I say enthusiastically. "She's going to make a great Belle. And, hey, guess who's playing the part of Beast?"

"Who?"

"Zach Norton. Remember him? From Little League last summer?"

"Oh, sure—Zach. That cute blond guy who played first base."

Megan stares out the window, her pale oval face a stony mask. Serves her right. Megan Wong and her friends may think they're in charge of the entire sixth grade, but that doesn't mean they are.

We round Monument Square, drive past the Hawthornes' house, and continue down Lowell Road to a part of town I haven't seen before. Book club is at Megan's house tonight, and she lives way out on Strawberry Hill.

"Is this it?" asks my mother, slowing down and peering at the street number on a big stone pillar that marks the entrance to a long driveway.

Megan nods.

"Wow," I say, catching a glimpse of her house through the leafless trees. It's huge and modern and looks like it's made entirely of glass. "It looks like a spaceship."

"Doesn't it," says my mother politely.

She's not crazy about modern architecture. "Old houses are the coziest," she always says. I think Mr. Hawthorne would probably agree with her. I overheard him talking about the Wongs' house at a barbecue last summer. "A carbuncle upon Concord's pastoral loveliness," he called it. I have no idea what a carbuncle is, but I could tell from his tone of voice that it wasn't something good.

I think the house is cool, though. And the inside is just as amazing as the outside. I try not to stare as Mrs. Wong takes our coats. Behind me, my mother is trying not to stare either. Megan's living room is seriously huge. Nearly as big as a hockey rink.

It's a weird shape, too, almost round. And it sticks right out into the middle of the yard, like an escape pod stuck onto the side of a spaceship. Too bad I can't push a button and fly myself home. The match between the Bruins and the Rangers will be starting soon on ESPN.

The phone rings and Mrs. Wong excuses herself. "Have a seat," she calls, disappearing down the hallway.

Jess and Mom and I step down into the room. My sneakers sink into the carpet nearly up to my ankles. It's white, and so is everything else in the room—sofas, chairs, carpets, walls. Even the baby grand piano is white. It's like being in the middle of a blizzard. I can't help it, it's just too tempting. *Push—glide, push—glide, push—glide.* I skim across the carpet like I'm flying down the rink, bodycheck a white leather chair with my hip, and spin around to see my mother glaring at me.

"Sorry," I mumble, dropping into the chair.

I sniff my armpit—passable, now that I have an almost-clean shirt on—and start to put my feet up on the coffee table in front of me. My

Heather Vogel Frederick

mother catches my eye and I hesitate. She reaches into her purse and pulls out a piece of paper, waving it in the air like a flag. It's Dr. Weisman's contract. I heave a sigh and put my feet on the floor instead. She nods, satisfied, and slips the contract back into her purse.

She and Jess sit down on the sofa. There's no sign of Megan. My mother is dressed all in red tonight—red pants, red sweater, red leather boots—and she stands out against all the white as vividly as a drop of blood on snow. Jess reaches out a tentative finger and strokes the clear glass Christmas tree that sits on the coffee table in front of them. I wonder if there's another, real tree somewhere in the house, or if this is it.

Mrs. Wong reappears. "We have a live tree out in a planter on the deck," she says, as if reading my thoughts. "The ornaments are made of birdseed. We'll plant it in the spring."

"Ah," says my mother, nodding. "An environmentally friendly Christmas." She looks around at the furnishings. "Your home is lovely."

"Thank you," Megan's mother replies. She waves a hand carelessly at the room. "Jerry picked everything out. I'm not much for decorating."

My mother looks surprised to hear this. Decorating is her life.

I can tell that she and Mrs. Wong are trying extra hard to be polite. They're getting along again finally, after the big blowup last month. Mrs. Hawthorne asked Mom and Mrs. Wong over to lunch to patch things up. I saw the invitation. It had a quote from Louisa May Alcott on the front: "Birds in their little nests agree." I guess they're trying to be good role models for us girls. My mother still hasn't been back to yoga class, though.

"That was Phoebe," says Mrs. Wong, glancing at her watch. "She and Emma should be here any minute. They're running a little late." She crosses to a small white speaker set into the wall and presses a button beneath it. "Megan!" she calls into it. "It's time to come join us! Your friends are waiting!"

I let out a snort. I am not Megan Wong's friend, and she's not mine. My mother gives me a warning look.

"I'll get the refreshments," says Mrs. Wong, and disappears again.

Jess cocks her head, turning her gaze from one side of the room to the other as if measuring it. "It's a dodecagon," she announces finally.

"A dodo-what?" I ask.

"A dodecagon," she repeats, as if that helps. "Twelve windows, see? Set at angles in nearly a perfect circle."

I stare around the room again. I have absolutely no idea what she's talking about. Of course, that's generally the case with Jessica Delaney. She never talks about regular stuff. I'll bet she doesn't even know who won the Stanley Cup last year.

I start gnawing at a hangnail. Unladylike, but necessary. Fortunately, the doorbell rings before my mother can start waving the contract at me again. Emma and her mother are here.

Emma makes a beeline for the sofa and plunks herself down next to Jess.

Heather Vogel Frederick

"Clementine!" says Mrs. Hawthorne brightly. "We've missed you at yoga."

My mother inclines her head regally, like a queen greeting a subject. She's going into full supermodel mode. She can still pull off world-famous "Clementine" when she needs to. "Things have been busy," she replies in a dignified tone.

Nobody mentions hockey.

Mrs. Wong comes in with a big platter piled high with lumpy gray cookies. "They're vegan," she says proudly, setting them down on the coffee table. "No eggs or animal fat. And the chips are carob, not chocolate."

"Yummy," says my mother, her forehead creasing with concern. I can't wait to watch Queen Clementine try and choke down one of those suckers. Next to decorating and gardening, baking is my mother's favorite activity. Courtney keeps telling her she should start her own TV show. She's probably right. They could call it "At Home with the Queen."

"Healthy treats are good treats," says Mrs. Hawthorne, but she doesn't look convinced either. I see her and Emma exchange a glance, and the corners of Mrs. Hawthorne's lips quirk up as she tries to suppress a smile. Emma's lucky—she and her mom are close. Kind of like my mother and my sister are. I know they love me, but it's sort of like they're this little twosome and I don't quite belong. I just don't have that much interest in nail polish and fashion magazines. *Any* interest, actually.

Mrs. Wong looks at her watch again and taps a foot impatiently. "Would you girls please go see if you can pry Megan out of her room? I don't know what's gotten into her tonight."

I follow Emma and Jess out of the living room and down an adjoining hall. A long, long hall. It's hard to believe that only three people live in this place. I've been in hotels that were smaller. I start skating again (push—glide, push—glide), and about a half a mile later we stop in front of a big white door.

"Megan?" Emma calls, tapping softly.

Pushing past her, I shove the door open and walk in. Like the rest of the house, Megan Wong's bedroom is huge. It juts out into the yard the same way the living room does. It's kind of like being in a tree house. I wouldn't mind a room like this, actually. Well, except for the furniture. Everything is pink and lacy, and the bed has one of those thingies draped over the top of it like a tent. I can't remember what they're called. No, wait a sec. A canopy. That's it. My mother would be delirious if she saw this room. It's like her dream girl's bedroom. Me? I would lie down on the floor and croak before I'd let her decorate my room like this. She wanted to get a canopy for my bed when I was little and I said absolutely not, no way. Too girly-girl. Give me a poster of Wayne Gretzky or Sarah Parsons and Team USA any day of the week.

"Hi," says Emma.

Megan whips around, startled. She must not have heard us come in. She shoves something hastily into her desk drawer. A notebook, maybe. "What do you want?" she demands.

Heather Vogel Frederick

"Um, your mom says it's time to come join us," says Emma.

"C'mon, Wong, you're holding up the show," I add. "The faster we get started, the faster we can get out of here." The Bruins match should be starting any second. With any luck, I can catch the second half.

Megan looks at me like I've got fleas. "It's your fault we're here in the first place," she says coldly. "If your mother hadn't changed her mind about dropping out of this stupid club, we wouldn't have to be here tonight at all."

"Just hurry up, will you?" I turn around to leave and nearly trip over Emma. She's kneeling on the carpet, smiling. In front of her is a plastic box of some kind she's pulled out from underneath Megan's bed.

"I didn't know you still had these!" she says, holding up a doll.

Megan flies across the room in about two seconds. She kicks the box back out of sight. "Don't touch my stuff!"

Emma recoils, like a goalie who's just had the stuffing knocked out of him. "Sorry," she whispers.

We head back to the living room in silence and take our seats. Mrs. Hawthorne—who has only taken a single bite out of her "healthy treat," I notice—calls the meeting to order.

"Did everybody get the reading done?" she asks.

Emma and Jess both nod. Megan shrugs. I don't say a word.

"Cassidy and I read this month's assignment together," says my mother, putting her arm around my shoulders and giving me a squeeze. "It was fun, wasn't it, sweetie?"

About as much fun as the time I got my nose broken with a hockey stick, I almost say, but I remember Dr. Weisman just in time and nod.

"Shall we talk about chapter 13?" says Mrs. Hawthorne. "That's one of my favorites."

As everyone opens their books, Megan leans toward me and takes a cookie from the plate. "Your mommy had to read the book to you?" she says in a mocking whisper. "Becca's right—you are a dumb jock."

I kick her in the shin. Hard. Mrs. Hawthorne glances over at us sharply. "Cassidy, why don't you begin by telling us what happens?"

I stare at the chapter heading and try to remember what the heck "Castles in the Air" was about. "Uh, it's a hot day, and Laurie finds the girls out in the woods knitting socks for the soldiers and stuff, and they get to talking about their dreams."

"What kinds of dreams?" coaxes Mrs. Hawthorne.

"Um, what they want to be when they grow up—stuff like that."

"Does anyone remember what those dreams are?"

Emma raises her hand. Of course. It's like she thinks we're at school or something.

"Yes, Emma?" says her mother.

"They all want to be rich and famous except Beth, who wants to stay home and take care of her mother and father.'"

Mrs. Hawthorne nods. "That's right. Let's read a little bit together, shall we?"

We dutifully read aloud the part where Laurie talks about being a famous musician when he grows up, and Meg tells them she

Heather Vogel Frederick

wants a big house and lots of money, and Jo says she wants to be a famous author, and Amy "the best artist in the whole world."

"How about you girls?" Mrs. Hawthorne asks us. "What are your dreams in life—your 'castles in the air'?"

We all sit in embarrassed silence. Finally, Mrs. Wong looks over at me. "How about you, Cassidy?" she prods. "What do you want to do with your life?"

"I want to play pro hockey," I mumble.

My mother bites her lip. Mrs. Wong and Mrs. Hawthorne nod thoughtfully, careful not to look at her. Hockey is still a sore spot.

"Anyone else?" asks Mrs. Wong.

"I'd like to be a writer," Emma admits shyly.

The mothers pounce on this safe response with relief.

"That's fabulous, Emma!" enthuses Mrs. Wong. "Writers can do so much good in the world. Maybe you'll grow up to be an investigative journalist and expose corruption."

Emma does not look terribly enthusiastic about this possibility.

"You picked a good town to grow up in, if you want to be a writer," says my mother, smiling at her. "Just think, our very own little Louisa!"

"I want to be a vet," says Jess out of the blue. Since she normally doesn't say anything at all at our meetings, the mothers instantly start gushing.

"Wow! That's great, honey!" says Mrs. Wong.

"Fabulous!" agrees my mother.

"You'd make an amazing veterinarian, Jess," adds Mrs. Hawthorne, beaming. "And you're getting a head start, too, by taking care of all the animals on your farm."

"Goat Girl," whispers Megan, and I kick her in the shin again. This time, she kicks me back.

Mrs. Hawthorne sees us and lifts an eyebrow. "How about you, Megan?" she asks. "Do you have any 'castles in the air'?"

Megan shrugs.

"Megan's going to be an environmental lawyer, aren't you, Megan?" Mrs. Wong prompts. She turns to look at the other mothers. "She'll go to MIT, like her dad and I did, and then we thought perhaps on to Harvard for law school."

Megan leans forward in her chair. She gazes intently at her mother with her dark, almond-shaped eyes. "I am not going to be an environmental lawyer," she says fiercely. "Ever. That's your 'castle in the air,' Mom. Not mine. I'm going to be a fashion designer."

This announcement is greeted with stunned silence. If Megan had said she wanted to be a rodeo cowboy we couldn't have been more surprised.

"You're too young to know what you want, sweetie," her mother says dismissively.

"But, Mrs. Wong, Megan's really good at sewing," blurts Emma. "She used to make the best clothes for our Barbies. She still has them, under her bed."

"I remember those clothes!" says Mrs. Hawthorne. "They were wonderful."

"Fashion is frivolous," Mrs. Wong objects.

Heather Vogel Frederick

"Not necessarily," says my mother, tapping the toe of her red leather boot against the coffee table. "I know a lot of fashion designers, and many of them are tremendously talented artists. It can be a great career."

"Not for my daughter," says Mrs. Wong, who is beginning to look a little steamed. "Fashion enslaves women. And really, ladies, after last month, I'm surprised I should have to remind you not to interfere in a family affair."

My mother and Mrs. Hawthorne exchange a guilty glance. I look over at Mrs. Wong and Megan. Mrs. Wong is wearing yoga pants and an "Imagine Whirled Peas" sweatshirt. Megan's outfit probably came straight off the pages of some teen magazine. I'll bet they fight about this stuff all the time—just like my mom and me, only the other way around.

"I don't necessarily think that all fashion is slavery," my mother says, her voice sounding clipped and tight. "It can be a form of self-expression, you know."

"Stay out of this, Clementine," Mrs. Wong warns.

"Shall we get back to *Little Women*?" Mrs. Hawthorne suggests, and gently steers the conversation away from touchy subjects like fashion and hockey. We talk about the book some more and scrape our teeth on Mrs. Wong's cookies, which are hard as rocks and taste just as bad as they look.

Finally, it's time for the handouts. I glance at my watch. Good. If we hurry, I can still catch the last period of the game.

Fun Facts About Louisa

1. Louisa kept a "mood pillow" shaped like a sausage on the parlor sofa. When she was in a good mood, she stood it on end. When she wasn't, she placed it flat, and her family gave her some space.

2. The Alcott family was very poor, and before she became a successful writer Louisa helped support her parents and sisters by working as a teacher, seamstress, governess, and household servant, and as a volunteer nurse during the Civil War.

3. In addition to books for young people, Louisa also wrote for adults. Sometimes she wrote under pseudonyms, including Flora Fairfield, Tribulation Periwinkle, and A. M. Barnard, under which alias she published what she called "blood and thunder" thrillers.

"How come we don't read one of those?" I ask. "'Blood and thunder' sounds a lot better than stupid *Little Women*."

My mother shoots me a look. Then she brightens. "You know," she says, "this discussion tonight has given me an idea."

Uh-oh, I automatically think. I know from experience that there's no telling what will happen when my mother gets an idea.

"Why don't we have a *Little Women* Christmas party?" she continues. "We could dress up in nineteenth-century fashions." She glances slyly at Mrs. Wong. "Fashion is an important part of history, after all. We can each

Heather Vogel Frederick

pick the character we think we're most like, and come dressed as her."

"What a marvelous idea!" cries Mrs. Hawthorne. "It sounds like great fun. Don't you think so, Lily?"

Mrs. Wong looks like she's trying to find a reason to disapprove, but finally she gives a reluctant nod. "I suppose so," she says.

"I'm too old to play dress-up," I tell them, trying to nip the plan in the bud. No way am I going to a party dressed as dumb Amy or Beth or any one of the sisters. Not even Jo. No way.

But it's too late. Mrs. Hawthorne and Mrs. Wong and my mother ignore me. The idea has caught fire.

"We can serve food from the book!" says my mother.

"The Alcotts were vegetarians," Mrs. Wong reminds us.

"But the March family wasn't," my mother counters.

Mrs. Hawthorne comes up with a compromise. "How about we make apple slump? That was one of the Alcotts' favorite desserts, plus it was Louisa's nickname for Orchard House."

"Why the heck did she call it that?" I ask.

"Because she had to spend so much money repairing it all the time," Mrs. Hawthorne tells me.

Mrs. Wong likes this idea. "I'll bring organic apples," she says happily. "Their food would have been organic back them. *Historically,* I mean," she adds, with a significant glance at my mother.

This is getting worse by the minute. I check my watch. Too late— the hockey game is over. I heave a sigh. Maybe it's not too late for me to weasel out of the party, though.

"We can have it at my house," my mother offers, looking around the living room. I know exactly what she's thinking. She's thinking that the Wongs and their dumb birdseed tree don't measure up in the holiday cheer department. Our house, on the other hand, looked like something out of a magazine by the day after Thanksgiving. It always does. "At Home with the Queen: The Holiday Special!"

My mother pulls her calendar out of her purse and scans it, frowning. "How about the Sunday afternoon before Christmas? Does that work for everyone? Plan to bring your families, of course."

Jess's face gets all anxious-looking, the way it does whenever anyone mentions her family. She probably feels the same way about her missing mother as I do about my dad. She has no reason to complain, though—at least her mom is still alive.

I stand up. "I just have one thing to say," I announce. Six pairs of eyes look at me expectantly. "No one, and I mean no one"—I glare at my mother—"is going to get me into a dress."

My mother smiles. She draws herself up into her regal supermodel pose. She reaches into her purse again, removes Dr. Weisman's contract, and waves it at me.

My first hockey game is a week away. I slump back down in the white leather chair. Resistance is futile. "Fine."

My mother inclines her head, looking pleased.

Final Score: Queen Clementine—1, Cassidy—0.

Heather Vogel Frederick

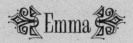# Emma

"I wish it was Christmas or New Year's all the time; wouldn't it be fun?"

I love snow days.

It's not fair when they happen during winter break, though. A real snow day means you get to miss school.

The storm started last night right before bedtime, the first flakes drifting down like tiny stars from the dark sky. It wasn't supposed to be a storm at all—only flurries were predicted. But something must have happened during the night, because when I woke up this morning and looked out my bedroom window our split-rail fence had vanished, and so had the mailbox and the road and all the shrubs in the front yard.

"Blizzard Breakfast!" my dad shouted up the stairs.

Dad always makes pancakes on snow days, and afterward Darcy and I always put on our snow gear and go outside. This morning we made snow angels and built a fort under the rhododendrons, just like we used to when we were little. Dad even came out and joined us for a snowball fight. He says a good snowstorm brings out the kid in everyone.

The only problem is that today is the day of our Little Women Christmas Party. Mom says that since it's still snowing we'll probably have to cancel, because the snowplows can't keep up and the roads are all blocked.

I have to admit I'm kind of disappointed. Mom and I baked gingerbread people for everyone and we bought long dresses at the thrift store to wear and everything.

Right now we're camped out in the living room, trying to stay warm. The electricity went off about an hour ago, along with the phones, and Dad built a roaring fire and closed off all the doors to keep the heat in. It's snug and peaceful, like Christmas morning, even though it's afternoon and Christmas is still a week away. Our tree is in the corner, and although the lights aren't working it looks pretty. It smells good, too, the satisfying aroma of evergreen mingling with the scent of wood smoke and wet wool from our mittens and hats sizzling themselves dry on the fireplace screen. My father is stretched out on the sofa reading a book about Thoreau that he's supposed to review, and my mom is wrapped in a quilt on the window seat rereading *Persuasion* (a Jane Austen novel, of course). Darcy and I are in our pajamas sprawled out on the hearth, playing Monopoly.

My mother's cell phone rings, and we all jump.

"Hello?" she says. "Yes, Clementine. Yes, I agree. There's really no other choice under the circumstances. Such a shame. Do you think we can reschedule for next week? It's such a fun idea, and I'm sure the girls are all really looking forward to it. I know Emma is."

Heather Vogel Frederick

She hangs up, and almost immediately the phone rings again. This time it's Mrs. Wong.

"Yes, Lily, I just got the news too," my mother says. "But we're going to try and reschedule. Clementine's calling the Delaneys right now. Are you staying warm enough out there? Oh, you do? Really? Wow, that's great."

"What's great?" asks my father when she hangs up.

"The Wongs have a generator, so everything's up and running."

"Figures," says my dad, a twinge of envy in his voice. He's been wanting a generator for a while now, but they're expensive, and besides, my mom always tells him, a generator is one of those things you only need once in a blue moon.

"But when the moon is blue, you sure wish you had one," Dad always counters.

Everything's quiet again for a while, then, just as Darcy puts a hotel on Park Place, the cell phone rings a third time. "Heavens, I'm the belle of the ball this afternoon!" says my mother. I can't tell who's on the other end of the line this time. "Uh-huh," she keeps repeating, then, "Nope, I won't breathe a word. Promise."

"Who was that?" I ask, curious.

"You'll see," she says loftily, which is mom-code for "I know something you don't and I'm not going to tell you."

"Come on, Mom," I wheedle.

She shakes her head and leaves the room, smiling to herself. I can hear her in the kitchen, rustling around. Something is definitely up.

"What's going on?" I ask my father.

"Haven't the foggiest," he replies, without looking up from his book. "Like your mother says, you'll see."

Parents can be so annoying sometimes.

A few minutes later, just as I'm about to collect double rent from Darcy for landing on Pennsylvania Railroad, my mother pokes her head back in the room. "You all need to get warm clothes on," she announces. "We'll be leaving soon."

"Leaving? For where?" I ask.

"The party, of course."

"But I thought it was cancelled."

My mother shakes her head. "Plans have changed—it's back on."

"How are we supposed to get there?" Darcy complains. He flaps his arms. "Fly?"

Mom smiles that smug smile again. "You'll see."

My father peers at her over the top of his book. "Let me guess," he says. "Jerry Wong rented a snowplow. No, wait—he *bought* a snowplow."

"Nicholas Hawthorne, behave yourself!" scolds my mother, but her eyes are twinkling so I can tell she's not really angry. "Jerry earned every cent of his money, and he has the right to spend it any way he wants to. Besides, don't forget all the charities they support. The Wongs are doing a great deal of good in this world."

Dad gets up off the sofa and kisses her cheek penitently. "You're right, as always," he says. "But for the record, I was just joking."

Mom swats him with a pair of mittens, which she then passes to me. "Put your warmest things on, okay? And make it snappy!"

By now I'm practically boiling over with curiosity. What has Mom got up her sleeve? Maybe Dad's right, maybe the Wongs really did buy a snowplow.

And then, in the distance, I hear something. A faint sound that is definitely not a snowplow. I run to the front window and look out. Lowell Road is still deserted. I hear the sound again. Bells? I frown, puzzled. A minute later my eyes nearly pop out of my head and the puzzle is solved when I spot Led and Zep, the Delaney's big Belgian draft horses, over the tops of the snowdrifts.

"It's a sleigh!" I cry in delight, running to the front door and throwing it open. "The Delaneys brought their sleigh!"

"Are you serious?" says Darcy, rushing to join me. Mom and Dad are right behind him. We all wave, and the Delaneys wave back.

None of us have ever ridden in a sleigh before. We watch, entranced, as Mr. Delaney pulls up across the street. The sleigh bells on the horses' harnesses really do jingle, just like in the Christmas carols.

"All aboard!" shouts Mr. Delaney.

We don't need to be asked twice. My brother grabs the duffel bag with our costumes in it and I grab the container with the gingerbread people and we skid down the front steps and the front walk and wade across the road through the snow. Jess and her brothers are in the back of the sleigh, huddled under mounds of blankets and sleeping bags. Jess scoots over and flips back a corner of one of the blankets.

"Can we all fit?" asks my mother.

"It'll be close quarters, but you'll stay warm," Mr. Delaney tells her. "When we get to the Wongs', maybe you can put Ryan on your lap, Jess, okay? And Darcy, I thought you might like to ride up here with me."

"No fair, Dad! I want to ride with you!" protests Dylan. Or maybe it's Ryan—even after five years I have a hard time telling them apart.

"You and your brother can take turns on the way home," Mr. Delaney promises. He waits until we're all seated, then flaps the reins. Led and Zep heave their way forward through the snow.

Slowly we pick up speed, and as the horses break into a slow trot and we begin to glide I suddenly feel giddy. I must be smiling because my mother is smiling back at me, and so are Dad and Jess. In fact, we're all smiling. Riding in a sleigh is magical. There's just the wind and the snow and the steady muffled clop of the horses' hooves and the hiss of the sleigh's runners and the rhythmic jangling of bells. It's like flying, only better.

"Now, this is the way to travel," says my mother dreamily, snuggling close to my dad. "I feel like a character out of one of Jane Austen's books."

My dad puts his arm around her. "Or *Little Women*," he adds, winking at me and Jess.

As we whiz along Lowell Road toward Strawberry Hill, I wonder if this is what the olden days felt like. If so, the olden days were a lot more fun than I imagined.

We reach the Wongs' driveway and there's Mr. Wong, sitting atop a small red snowplow. He waves happily at us and toots the horn.

"See?" my father whispers to my mother. "I told you so."

My mother giggles, which is not a sound she usually makes. She sounds—well, like a girl. My dad is right. Snowstorms do bring out the kid in everyone.

"Perfect timing!" shouts Mr. Wong. "I just finished clearing a path— I'll go and get Lily and Megan!"

A couple of minutes later the Wongs appear and we all shove over to make room for them.

"Hey, Megs," says my brother, who is one of the few people who can call Megan by her kindergarten nickname and get away with it.

"Hey," she replies, giving him a quick smile. For a brief second I see a flash of the old Megan, the pre-Fab Four Megan. The Megan I still miss and wish I had back for a friend. Just as quickly, though, the smile disappears, leaving in its place the Megan who isn't interested in being my friend. The Megan who let Becca Chadwick read my journal out loud.

As the sleigh pulls forward again, Megan avoids looking at me and Jess and fiddles with her cell phone instead. I figure she's probably text messaging the Fab Four, telling them what a stupid idea this is, but for once I don't let it bother me. I pull the blankets up under my chin and watch the snow drift down over the fields and trees and stone walls that give way to houses as we draw closer to town.

"A real blast from the past you have here, Michael!" Mr. Wong calls to Mr. Delaney, who turns around in the driver's seat and smiles at us.

"I thought you'd like it," he replies. "Historically accurate, too. For the party, I mean. This sleigh's over a hundred years old." He waggles his eyebrows at his boys. "Almost as old as I am."

The twins snicker.

As we approach town, people spot us and actually come out of their houses to wave and cheer us on. I guess it's not every day you see a sleigh driving through the streets of Concord, Massachusetts.

"Look, dear, there's Calliope Chadwick," says my father, pointing to the doorway of a huge white colonial-style house.

My mother grits her teeth in a smile. "Merry Christmas!" she calls.

Mrs. Chadwick starts to wave, then sees that it's us. She scowls and goes back inside, slamming the door.

"Ah, the Christmas spirit," says my father. "Such a beautiful thing."

The grown-ups all laugh.

"I'll bet this is just what everything looked like when the Alcotts lived here," Jess whispers.

I nod. "Pretty, isn't it?"

Mr. Delaney starts to hum "Jingle Bells," and my mom quickly picks up the tune. Soon, we're all singing—all except for Megan, who's still busy with her cell phone.

Snow sifts down, but more slowly now. The blizzard is finally dying out. We sing all the way down Monument Street, past houses lit by candlelight and past the Colonial Inn and past the festive storefronts of Main Street. We're still singing as we pull up in front of the Sloanes' house. Their front door flies open and Cassidy comes shooting out like a cannonball. Her mother and sister are right behind her.

"No fair!" Cassidy shouts. "I want a ride!"

"Hop in," Mr. Delaney tells her as the rest of us all climb out. "I'll take you for a spin around the block."

"Go ahead inside and get warm," says Mrs. Sloane as she steps into the sleigh. "Well, sort of warm. The electricity's still out, but I managed to get a fire going in the living room."

Mr. Delaney passes a bulging backpack down to Darcy. "I brought our old camp stove," he tells Cassidy's mother. "Figured we could make cocoa this way. And there's fresh goat's milk in case you're out of the regular stuff."

"Goat Girl," Megan whispers to Jess, low enough so that the grown-ups can't hear.

"Shut up, Megan," I whisper back. I take Jess's mittened hand and squeeze it.

"Oh, and there are hot dogs and buns, and marshmallows, too," Mr. Delaney adds. "And the apples that Lily wanted."

"Perfect! Thank you, Michael," Mrs. Sloane says, and there's a chorus of "thank you's" from the rest of the grown-ups. Mr. Delaney flaps the reins. The sleigh glides away.

Inside, the living room has been transformed.

"Wow!" says Jess, looking around in wonder. "It looks just like the movie. *Little Women*, I mean."

"No kidding," I reply. Everything looks old-fashioned and perfect.

The mantel is fringed with boughs of evergreen, and so is the top of the piano and all the end tables. Mrs. Sloane has woven clusters of red holly berries and lengths of plaid ribbon through them, and everywhere I look, there are candles. The room is practically glowing.

"Clementine sure has a knack for decorating," says my mother.

My dad and Darcy get right to work on beefing up the fire, and Mr. Wong heads for the back porch with the camp stove. Meanwhile, Jess and I help Mrs. Wong and my mother set out the food. Ryan and Dylan raid the gingerbread cookies the minute our backs are turned, then scamper off with their booty to explore the house. We can hear their footsteps running up and down the stairs, and their shouts of glee when they discover the turret.

By the time Mr. Delaney gets back with the Sloanes, the cocoa is ready.

"Everything looks gorgeous, Clementine," says my mother, handing her a mug of the steaming, fragrant drink. "Especially your tree. Are the ornaments antique?"

"They are," Mrs. Sloane replies. "I've collected them for years. David"—she hesitates slightly, then continues—"my husband used to give me one every year. His job took him all over the world, and he was always finding beautiful things."

"He sounds like a wonderful man," says my mother quietly, patting her shoulder.

Mrs. Wong appears carrying a platter of hot dog buns. "Thank goodness they're whole wheat," she says, eyeing them askance. "You don't by any chance have tofu dogs, do you?"

Heather Vogel Frederick

Mrs. Sloane and my mother exchange a glance. "Sorry, we're fresh out," says Mrs. Sloane.

"What do you say we all get into our costumes?" my mother suggests, distracting Mrs. Wong from the menu's failings.

Jess and Megan and I follow Cassidy upstairs with our things. I look around her room curiously. Her bookcases are stuffed not with books but with sports trophies, and the walls are covered with posters of hockey and baseball players.

"This one's signed," she says proudly, pointing to a picture of someone named Wayne Gretzky. "My dad gave it to me for my birthday two years ago."

"Big deal," says Megan. "Who cares about a stupid hockey player."

"Wayne Gretzky isn't a stupid hockey player!" Cassidy cries hotly. "He's called The Great One, and he's the most famous player in the history of the sport!"

Megan shrugs, unimpressed.

We change out of our warm things and pull our dresses on. Jess and Cassidy and I help each other with our zippers. Megan manages on her own. Cassidy leaves her sweatpants and sneakers on underneath her long dress, but the rest of us put on tights and fancier shoes.

"May I have your attention, please!" Mrs. Sloane says dramatically as we troop back down to the living room. She looks gorgeous, of course, in a floor-length red-and-green-plaid taffeta dress that makes her look like a life-sized Christmas ornament. My parents and Megan's parents and Mr. Delaney and Darcy and Courtney and the twins all turn around to see what's going on. "I'd like to present our own little women!"

Our families break into applause as the four of us straggle rather anticlimactically into the living room. Ryan and Dylan run around the room in excitement, hitting each other with sofa pillows.

"Boys!" scolds Mr. Delaney. "Knock it off!"

"Line up in front of the fireplace," Mrs. Sloane tells us, and we slouch together into a stiff group. Her camera flashes and everyone applauds again.

"Now," says my mother, whose long, faded thrift store calico looks like a relic from *Little House on the Prairie,* "why don't you tell us who you are?"

We look at each other, embarrassed, then stare at our feet.

"Come on," prods Mrs. Wong. "Megan, you go first."

Megan shoots her mother a resentful glance. "I'm Amy," she mumbles.

"Ah, the artist," says my mother, nodding sagely. "Of course. Excellent choice. How about you, Jess?"

Jess's voice is so low we can hardly hear her. "I'm Beth," she replies softly.

"The animal lover!" says Mrs. Sloane.

"Goat Girl," whispers Megan.

"And the musician, too," adds my mother. "Very appropriate."

"How about you, Emma?" asks Mrs. Wong. "Who are you?"

"Jo," I tell her. "Because I want to be a writer."

My father beams at me. "Like father, like daughter," he says proudly.

Heather Vogel Frederick

Mrs. Sloane, who is standing next to him, frowns. "I thought you'd choose Meg," she says.

I shake my head. "Nope," I tell her. "I'm Jo."

"But Cassidy is Jo," she protests. "We need a Meg!"

Everyone looks over at Cassidy, who folds her arms defiantly across her chest. "Mom wouldn't let me be Laurie," she says.

"Who's Laurie?" asks my brother. "I thought there were only four sisters."

"Laurie is a boy," my mother replies.

"A boy named Laurie?" my brother sounds incredulous. "How lame is that?"

"Actually, he's Theodore Laurence," says my mother. "The March girls call him Laurie for short."

"Except girls back then wouldn't wear this," says Megan, her hand darting out. She hoists up the hem of Cassidy's dress, revealing the sweatpants and sneakers underneath. Everybody laughs. Cassidy twitches her dress away angrily.

"Actually," says my mother, "that's exactly what Jo *would* do. She was a tomboy, remember? Just like Louisa."

"So we don't have a Meg?" asks Mrs. Sloane, still looking dismayed.

"It's okay if we have two Jo's, Clementine," says my mother soothingly. "Really, it's okay."

"How about if I'm half Jo, half Meg?" I volunteer. It is Christmas, after all.

Mrs. Sloane brightens. "Oh, good!" she says, relieved. "Now we can take the other picture."

She arranges us in a pose that looks just like the Jessie Wilcox Smith illustration on the cover of our journals. Jess sits on a chair, and I stand behind her between Megan and Cassidy. "Perfect!" says Mrs. Sloane, and her camera flashes again.

"How about you three visions of loveliness?" asks my father. "Who are you supposed to be?"

My mother and Mrs. Wong and Mrs. Sloane all look at each other.

"I, uh—"

"Are you—"

"Well, I—"

They all speak at once, then stop, flustered. My mother turns to my father. "I think we all came dressed as Marmee," she tells him, laughing.

He laughs too. "Naturally! The perfect mother. Which you all are, of course."

I look them over. Maybe my dad is right, maybe there's a little bit of Marmee in all of them. But I can't helping thinking that my own mother is the most Marmee-like. Beside me, Jess shifts uncomfortably. Mr. Delaney pokes busily at the fire. I wonder if they're thinking about Mrs. Delaney. Would she have come dressed as Marmee too?

"Now, boys," says Mrs. Sloane to my brother and the Delaney twins, "how about you start roasting hot dogs for us?"

While they're busy doing that, we spread an old quilt out in front of the fireplace and get to work making the apple slump. In a flash Mrs. Sloane has us peeling apples, chopping nuts, and mixing ingredients. Courtney brings an old-fashioned kettle from the kitchen, which my dad carefully hangs from an iron hinge on the fireplace. He swings it into position over the fire. Megan and Cassidy add in water, sugar, and cinnamon.

"Pop the apples in when they're ready," Mrs. Sloane instructs the grown-ups. She turns to Jess and me. "How are you coming along with the dough?"

"Almost done," I tell her, as Jess and I sift together the rest of the dry ingredients. "You can add the milk, Jess."

She carefully pours it in, and I stir everything together. "Ready!"

The apple slices are boiling now in the sugar water, and Mrs. Sloane drops spoonfuls of dough on top of them. She puts a cover on the kettle and swings it back over the fire. "Should be ready in half an hour," she tells us.

"Everybody ready for hot dogs?" asks Darcy, placing a heaping platter of them in the middle of the quilt.

"What a feast!" says Mr. Wong, digging in.

"Even if it's not historically accurate," jokes my father.

"Or organic," adds Mrs. Wong regretfully. "Well, except for the apple slump."

Mr. Delaney wipes his hands on his jeans. He clears his throat. "Um, Shannon wanted me to tell you that she wishes she could be here today. Since she wasn't able to, she sent along some presents for everyone."

"That's so sweet of her!" says my mother. She puts her arm around Jess and gives her a squeeze. "You have such a wonderful mother."

Jess's eyes fill with tears. Poor thing. Her mother is staying in New York for the holidays. She sent train tickets for Jess and her brothers, and they'll spend Christmas at Half Moon Farm and then travel down to New York for New Year's. It's not the same, though. Jess was really hoping that her mother would have come home by now.

Mr. Delaney reaches into his backpack and distributes some packages. There are books about historical Concord for all the fathers, and bags of penny candy for the older kids and for the twins. "And these are for the members of the Mother-Daughter Book Club," he says, handing us each a flat book with a bookmark stuck inside.

"*Little Women* paper dolls?" cries Cassidy in disgust. "What am I supposed to do with these?"

"Cassidy!" says her mother sharply. "Manners, please."

Cassidy heaves a dramatic sigh. She turns to Mr. Delaney. "Please tell Mrs. Delaney that the paper dolls are great!" she chirps. "Just what I wanted!"

Mrs. Sloane shakes her head. "Hopeless," she says wearily. "Just hopeless."

I pull out my bookmark. On it is a quote from Louisa May Alcott: "I am not afraid of storms, for I am learning how to sail my ship." Somehow I don't think she's talking about sailing. She's talking about life. I read the quote again. I like it.

Heather Vogel Frederick

Across the quilt from me, Megan is inspecting the paper dolls. "They didn't get these dresses right," she says.

"How do you know that?" her mother asks.

"Oh, some book about fashion history I found at the library. That Mrs. Hawthorne helped me find, I mean."

Mrs. Wong frowns, and my mother looks sheepish.

Megan turns her attention back to the paper dolls. I watch her for a minute, then suddenly I get a flash of inspiration.

"Mrs. Sloane, do you have any colored pencils and paper we could use?" I ask.

"Sure, honey," she replies, pointing to a desk across the room. "Third drawer down."

I retrieve them and put them in front of Megan, who is still scrutinizing the book. "If the dresses in there are wrong," I say hesitantly, "why don't you draw some that are right?"

Megan glances up at me through a wing of dark hair that's partially obscuring her face. I can't read her expression. She looks down again. Her fingers wander over to the pencils almost automatically. Without a word she picks one up, and in a flash her hand is moving swiftly over the paper and she's completely absorbed, just the way she used to be when she was designing clothes for our Barbies.

Hope flutters inside me as I watch her draw. It's the old Megan, the pre-Fab Four Megan. I haven't seen her like this since the last time we played at her old condo. Back in fourth grade, before that awful summer when she decided Becca and Ashley and Jen were cooler than me and we stopped being friends.

Megan finishes and hands me a piece of paper. I look down at the dress that she's sketched.

"Wow," I tell her. "This is amazing."

Megan smiles. A real Megan smile, not a fake wannabe one. I smile back.

"It's okay if you like that sort of thing," adds Cassidy, craning over my shoulder to see. Her mother gives her a sharp look and mouths a word. "Contact," maybe, or "contract"? Cassidy sighs. "I mean, yeah, cool. Good job, Megan."

"I love it!" I tell Megan, and I mean it. I grab the scissors and cut it out. The pink gown that she's drawn fits my paper doll perfectly. Over on the sofa, Mrs. Wong watches us, a thoughtful look on her face.

Courtney comes over to take a peek. She whistles. "Mom, you've got to see this!" she says, whisking the paper doll away from me and passing it to her mother.

Mrs. Sloane's eyes widen as she examines the pink dress. "Megan, they're right—this dress is gorgeous," she says. "You have real talent. When you get older, if you're still interested, there are fashion designers I'd love to introduce you to."

Megan smiles again—another real, honest-to-goodness Megan smile. "I could make accessories for them, too," she offers shyly. The flutter of hope inside me is now waving like a flag. Maybe the real Megan is still in there somewhere, like a chick trapped inside its shell, not sure how to peck its way out.

Maybe there's a way we could still be friends.

And then my mother ruins everything.

"Say, Megan," she says, "I heard Mrs. Adams talking at the PTA meeting right before school got out, and she's needing help with costumes for the play. I know you're busy learning your part, but maybe you'd be willing to help out in the design department?" She smiles over at Jess. "Our Jess—I mean our Belle—is going to need a spectacular ballgown for the final scene. How about a Wong original?"

At the mention of the play, Megan's smile disappears. She shoots Jess a swift glance, sharp as a needle, and puts her pencil down.

With a sinking heart I realize that I'm not getting my old friend back for Christmas. No way. The Christmas truce is over.

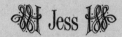 Jess

*"What do girls do who haven't any mothers
to help them through their troubles?"*

"So were you this nervous on your first opening night?"

My mother doesn't answer. She never does. How could she? She's just an image on the TV screen.

It's not that we don't talk on the phone—we do. She's really good about calling me and my brothers every few days, but still, it's not the same as having her here with us at home. Watching her on *HeartBeats* is the best I can do for now. It feels good to see her face and hear her voice, and for a few minutes I can pretend that she's in the same room with me.

Onscreen, Mom is batting her eyes at the actor who plays her true love, Judd Chance. He looks like he's been chiseled out of granite. People in real life never look like the people on TV. There's certainly nobody in Concord who looks like Judd Chance. Not that I've seen, anyway. He must be from California.

"I'm so afraid I'm going to panic when the curtain goes up," I tell her. "Did you ever feel that way?"

My mother is staring rapturously into Judd's impossibly handsome face.

"Larissa," he murmurs. "My love."

"Oh, my darling!" she replies. "Whatever shall we do?"

Sugar, who is sitting on the bed beside me, pricks up her ears and wags her tail when she hears Mom's voice.

"Sorry, girl," I tell her, turning the volume down. No need to listen to this drivel.

I bite into an apple. "I don't know what you and Judd are going to do, but I'm worried I might faint or something," I continue. "I really wish you could be here tonight."

My mother was supposed to come home to Concord this weekend to see the play. But then *HeartBeats* got nominated for some big award—which is hard to believe, because it's really, truly the most ridiculous show imaginable—and the awards ceremony is this weekend and the whole cast is supposed to attend, so she couldn't get away.

She and Dad got into a big argument over it on the phone, which I wasn't supposed to hear but how could I help it? Dad was yelling at her that she was selfish and from what I could gather she was yelling back at him that this was a big opportunity for her and that he was being the selfish one.

On my dresser is a huge bouquet of flowers. Mom sent them after the argument. They arrived while I was at school, along with a note apologizing that she wasn't able to be here for the play. She said she hoped I'd understand, and she sent me another train ticket, too, for spring break in New York. To make it up to me.

I take another bite of apple. I'm trying not to care that Mom can't come, but I can't help it. I do care. I really want her here with me.

By now, Mom and her TV boyfriend are in a passionate clinch. In addition to stupid dialogue, there's a lot of kissing on soap operas. Even though I know it's just acting, it's weird to see Mom kissing somebody besides Dad. I'm glad I don't have to kiss anybody in *Beauty and the Beast*. It's hard enough having to waltz around the stage with Zach Norton with everybody watching.

"So here's the thing," I say to my mother. "What if I'm terrible? What if everybody laughs when I open my mouth to sing? I'll just die if that happens, I know it."

Mom doesn't reply, of course. I look longingly at the phone. There's no point trying to call her. She's at the salon right now getting ready for the awards ceremony. I know this because she told me so when we talked briefly this morning, before school. She called to wish me luck—to "break a leg," as they say in show business. I made her promise she'd call me again later, after her awards ceremony, no matter how late it was, so I could tell her all about opening night.

The phone rings. My heart leaps. My mother read my thoughts!

But it's just Emma.

"So are you ready for tonight?" she asks me.

"Ready to throw up," I tell her.

She laughs. "Jess, you're gonna be great. I've been to nearly every rehearsal. Trust me."

Heather Vogel Frederick

Emma ended up volunteering to be assistant director. That means she's in charge of props, and making sure everything's where it should be backstage, and that all the actors get onstage when they're supposed to.

"My mom says to tell your dad we're on our way to get the pizzas, and that he should drop you off here at four thirty," she continues.

"Okay."

We're having an opening night party at the Hawthornes' tonight, before the show. I'll probably be too nervous to eat, even though we're going to have an early dinner since Megan and I have to be at school by six to get into our costumes and warm up.

I groan and flop onto my back on the bed. "What have I gotten myself into, mom?" I ask the TV screen.

My mother looks straight at the camera and smiles. I sit up. "It's not funny! I'm serious! I can't go through with this!"

But *HeartBeats* is over, and the screen goes black. I wait to see the credits before I turn off the TV. I always like to see my mother's name. There it is: Shannon O'Halloran as Larissa LaRue. My mother is using her maiden name as her stage name, just like she did years ago when she and Dad were first married. It's hard to imagine my parents living in New York City, but they did. Mom was an actress way back then, before Dad inherited the farm. A good actress, too, Dad says. Unlike me, who is going to bomb.

I shove thoughts of tonight's impending disaster aside and work on homework until it's time to leave. Ryan and Dylan pile into the back seat of the pickup truck, kicking and chopping at each other. Dad is taking them to karate lessons after dropping me at the Hawthornes'. When we get to Emma's house, he leans over and gives me a hug.

"I'll see you at school," he says. "Your brothers and I will be sitting with the Hawthornes. Phoebe got us all seats in the front row."

"Okay."

"You're going to be a beautiful Belle, honey."

"Thanks, Dad." I kiss his cheek, then climb out of the truck. "Don't forget to pick up Sundance."

Sundance is my pet goat. She's a little Nubian I raised for a 4-H project last spring, and she started limping a few days ago so we took her to the vet.

"Don't worry, I won't." He toots three times on the horn as he drives away, our family's "I love you" code.

The Hawthornes' house smells wonderfully of pizza, which I normally adore, but tonight, as I suspected, I can hardly eat a thing. Neither can Megan, I notice, and I almost ask her if she's nervous about opening night too, but I don't. She'll just say something mean like she always does. She's hardly said two words to me since I got picked for the part of Belle. She's said plenty to everybody else, though. She and Becca have spread the rumor all over school that the only reason I got cast is because my mother left and the drama teacher feels sorry for me. Emma says let them talk, just wait until I open my mouth and sing, that'll shut them up.

But what if I open my mouth to sing tonight and nothing at all comes out? Or worse, what if too much comes out? What if I croak like a frog? Or throw up?

While I'm picking at my pizza imagining all the horrible fates that await me onstage, Mr. Hawthorne arrives home from hockey practice with Darcy and Cassidy. The three of them cram in around the dining room table with the rest of us and Darcy and Cassidy proceed to wolf down an entire pizza between the two of them.

"Goodness," says Mrs. Wong, who is nibbling at some brown rice stir-fry thing she brought in a plastic container. "You two must be hungry."

"Starved," says Cassidy. She takes a big swig of root beer and belches.

Her mother looks shocked. "Cassidy Ann!"

Cassidy grins sheepishly. "Excuse me."

Beside me, I notice Megan pull out her cell phone and start text messaging surreptitiously under the table. She sees me watching and glares. I stare back down at my pizza.

"Louisa May would certainly approve of tonight's performance," says Mrs. Hawthorne. "She was quite an actress herself. And a playwright."

"Didn't I read someplace that she had a play produced in Boston once?" asks Mr. Hawthorne.

"You sure did," Mrs. Hawthorne replies. "And she did a lot of acting, too, both as an adult and while she was growing up. She and her sisters made all their own props and costumes, just like the March girls in *Little Women*. Remember Roderigo's boots?"

"Hmmm," muses Mr. Hawthorne. "The ones on display at Orchard House, right?"

Mrs. Hawthorne nods. "Louisa designed and sewed them for one of their plays."

Across the table from me, a flicker of interest crosses Megan's face.

Mrs. Sloane looks at the two of us and smiles. "And now we have our two budding actresses right here. You girls are going to be wonderful tonight, I just know it."

"Especially Jess," says Emma, beaming at me.

"Don't forget Megan," says Mrs. Hawthorne, winking at her. "She's quite the dish."

Everybody laughs at her little joke, except Megan, who glares stonily at her pizza.

"But Jess is the main course," says Cassidy, mumbling the words through a mouthful of pizza. Mrs. Sloane frowns and shakes her head sternly. Cassidy chews vigorously and swallows, then opens her mouth wide to show her mother that it's empty. Mrs. Sloane throws her hands in the air. "I give up," she says, and all the parents laugh.

We talk for a while more, and then it's time to leave. I'm driving with the Sloanes, and as we head for their minivan, my legs feel like lead. I'm very, very glad that I didn't eat much. When we talked on the phone this morning, Mom said everybody feels this way right before a performance, but that once I get out onstage it'll be fine. I find that hard to believe. Impossible, in fact.

At school, I follow Mrs. Sloane to a classroom that's been set up for

Heather Vogel Frederick

hair and makeup. She volunteered to be in charge of all that.

"Why don't you change into your costume for the first scene and then I'll work my magic," she tells me, plugging in a curling iron.

I head for the girls' room, and by the time I return she's putting the finishing touches on the Fab Four.

"I hate this costume so much," says Megan, examining herself in the mirror. She's wearing a black bodysuit, and she's sandwiched between two huge round pieces of cardboard that have been spray-painted gold. Becca, Ashley, and Jen are dressed the same, except that Becca's cardboard cutouts are in the shape of a cup, and Ashley's and Jen's are a knife and fork.

"Nonsense, you girls look great," Mrs. Sloane tells her. "Just the way royal dishes should look."

Megan makes a face at herself in the mirror. Becca, Ashley, and Jen do the same.

"Monkey see, monkey do," I mutter.

Emma pokes her head in the door. "Warm-up in five!" she calls, then disappears again.

Mrs. Sloane turns to me. As she starts curling my hair, another head pops in through the doorway. It's Zach Norton.

"Is it safe to come in?"

Mrs. Sloane nods.

He crosses the room and hands me a single red rose. "This is for you," he says shyly. "Good luck tonight. I mean, break a leg."

"You, too, Zach," I reply. "Thanks." In the mirror's reflection I can see the Fab Four watching us. Megan looks like she's wishing the floor would open and swallow me up. Too bad, I think. It's her own dumb fault that Zach is keeping his distance. She shouldn't have let Becca read Emma's poem at the rink.

Zach tugs on one of my long blonde ringlets. "Nice look."

"Thanks," I say again.

As he turns to leave, Calliope Chadwick barges into the room. She grabs Becca by the arm and hauls her over to Mrs. Sloane.

"My daughter needs more glitter!" she orders.

Mrs. Sloane puts down the curling iron. "I think Becca has enough glitter on her face," she replies.

"The audience will hardly be able to see her! I want her to shine!"

"Don't forget that Becca only has a supporting role, Calliope," says Mrs. Sloane, smiling sweetly. "Members of the chorus aren't supposed to outshine the star."

Becca goes back over to join her friends, and Mrs. Chadwick casts a sour glance at me. Behind her, the door opens and my father comes in. "Star?" she says to Mrs. Sloane. "Ha! From what I've heard, the casting of this play was influenced by favoritism, and I plan to speak to the school board about it. Giving lead roles to hoity-toity girls from some ramshackle farm who think they're something special just because they're in some ridiculous book club, and just because their mothers happen to be acting in some ridiculous soap opera, is no way to run a drama department."

"That ramshackle farm, as you call it, has been around since the

Heather Vogel Frederick

Revolutionary War," my father says quietly. Mrs. Chadwick whirls around, surprised to see him there. "In case you've forgotten, Calliope, Paul Revere himself took shelter there with one of my ancestors, while your in-laws were busy turning traitor."

The Revolutionary War is a sore spot with Mrs. Chadwick, whose husband's family sided with the British.

"And from what I've heard," my father continues in that ultracalm voice he uses when he's furious, "your daughter got just the role she deserved. I hear she's pretty good at *dishing* out unkindness."

Mrs. Chadwick's mouth pops open in an angry *O*. Before she can say anything, Mrs. Sloane slaps something into her hand. "You want glitter?" she says frostily. "Take the glitter. Just remember, though, all that glitters is not gold. And that includes dancing tableware."

Mrs. Chadwick gives a wounded sniff, draws herself up with as much dignity as she can muster, and waddles off. Her attempt at a grand exit is spoiled, however, by her large bottom, which wags behind her like a reproachful buffalo.

"Don't pay any attention to that old battleax," my father tells me once she's out of earshot. "You earned this role fair and square. And besides that, you look like a princess!"

I give him a sidelong glance. "Princess Jess of Ramshackle Farm?"

Mrs. Sloane laughs. "That's the spirit."

"Is Sundance okay?" I ask my father.

He nods. "You bet. She's in her crate in the back of the truck."

"Who's Sundance?" asks Mrs. Sloane, winding another strand of my hair around the curling iron.

"My pet goat," I explain. "She was at the vet's."

Across the room, I hear the Fab Four burst into laughter. I don't even have to look at them to know they're talking about me. *Goat Girl,* they're saying. I feel my face grow hot.

My dad gives me a kiss and tells me to break a leg, and then it's time for warm-ups and a pep talk by Mrs. Adams. As we take our places backstage, Emma peeks through the curtains. "It's filling up!" she reports. I pace back and forth, wiping the palms of my hands on my dress and trying in vain to control the wild thudding of my heart.

The prelude starts and Emma shoves a book into my hands. I stare at it blankly.

"Your prop for the first scene, remember?" she whispers.

I try and recall the first scene. I can't. I try and recall my first line—nothing! I grab her arm, panicked.

"You're gonna be great," she reassures me, and races off.

The curtain rises and the audience claps enthusiastically when they see our elaborate stage set—the painted wooden houses and storefronts of a small French village. I peer out from the wings and spot my father and my brothers sitting next to Darcy and Emma's parents in the front row, right where they said they'd be. I look around for my mother, just in case maybe she decided to surprise me, but she's nowhere in sight.

The first number begins and Mrs. Adams pokes me in the back, my

Heather Vogel Frederick

cue for my entrance. I take a deep breath and wander out onstage, pretending to read a book like I'm supposed to. I focus on the music and try to ignore the audience. *The stage fright will pass,* I tell myself grimly. Mom promised.

Amazingly, astonishingly, she was right. As soon as I open my mouth and begin to sing, suddenly I'm not me anymore, and this isn't the stage at Walden Middle School in Concord, Massachusetts. I've been transported to a village in France, and I am Belle. I have actually become her. Jess— shy, tongue-tied Jess—is someplace far, far away. There's only the music and me and the audience, who is hanging on my every note.

I'm soaring.

Is this how it is for Mom, a distant part of my mind wonders? Does she feel this way when she's acting too? This alive? Is this why she had to leave Half Moon Farm? To feel this incredible feeling again? But this isn't the time or place for such thoughts and I shove them away, forcing myself to concentrate instead on the action onstage.

We're almost through the first act when it happens. Right at the end of a big, rousing number, the one where the dishes and furniture from the Beast's castle break into song for Belle. I don't notice that all the dishes aren't there, that a certain cup has disappeared offstage, and I don't notice the commotion a short while later in the wings when the cup returns. I hear a ripple of laughter from the audience and assume it's because of the tableware cancan line. That always gets a laugh.

But the ripple becomes a tidal wave and the music grinds to a halt and I turn around to see a goat skitter across the stage.

"Sundance?" I whisper, incredulous. "How did you get out of the truck?"

My pet's left foreleg is wrapped tightly in a white bandage and she's limping. She spots me and comes trotting over.

"Maaaa-aaaa," she bleats.

The audience hoots with laughter.

Sundance butts her head softly against me. "Maaa-aaaa," she bleats again, her sweet little voice muffled by the fabric of my long dress. But it can't muffle her fear. She's scared by all the lights and people.

"Goat Girl," calls Megan in a stage whisper, and she and the Fab Four start to laugh. So does the rest of the cast. Mrs. Adams chooses this unfortunate moment to rush onto the stage waving her clipboard, which startles Sundance. Sundance takes off again, and pretty soon all the boys in the cast are chasing her and all the girls are scattering, their squeals blending with my pet's frantic bleats.

"Leave her alone!" I cry. "She's scared!"

No one can hear me above the pandemonium. No one but Sundance, that is. She tries to dodge a couple of villagers to reach me, but one of them grabs hold of her tail as she darts past and she stumbles and falls.

"You're hurting her! *Stop it!*" I scream.

"Go, Goat Girl!" cries Becca, and she and the Fab Four break into an impromptu cancan. The audience loves it. No one's paying the least bit of attention to me.

Heather Vogel Frederick

It's Darcy Hawthorne who saves the day. He jumps up onto the stage from the front row just as Sundance wobbles back up onto her legs and makes another bid for freedom. Standing quietly till she scoots past, he throws his coat over her and whisks her up in his arms.

I rush over to them both, sobbing.

"It's okay, Jess, it's okay," Darcy assures me. "I've got her—she's safe."

Mrs. Adams gestures frantically at Emma and the backstage crew and the curtain comes down, mercifully concealing my humiliation from the flabbergasted audience.

And as it does, all I can think is, *I'm so glad my mother wasn't here to see this.*

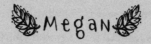

Megan

*"The storm cleared up below, for Mrs. March came home,
and having heard the story, soon brought Amy to a sense
of the wrong she had done her sister."*

I still don't get what the big deal is.

I mean, it was just a joke, for Pete's sake! You can't tell me they did-n't think it was funny—everyone thought it was funny. The whole audience cracked up. And it's not like it ruined the play or anything. Once Darcy and Mr. Delaney put Jess's goat back in the truck, we just started the scene over and everything was fine. But you'd think I was some kind of a criminal, the way people have been treating me. I'm grounded for the rest of the month, and Mrs. Adams yanked Becca and me out of the play when she found out we were behind "the goat stunt," as she put it. Zach Norton and the other boys are barely talk-ing to us, and of course Emma and Cassidy are making a point of ignoring us as well. As for Jess—well, Jess just mopes around like she always does, looking all hurt and wounded. She practically cringes every time I walk by, like maybe I'm going to hit her or something. It's all so stupid. And so unfair. Becca says everyone's way overreacting, and I agree.

"I expect your full cooperation tonight," says my mother.

We're on our way to the library. I've been temporarily paroled from house arrest for an emergency session of the Mother-Daughter Book Club. My mother is worried I'm going to get kicked out. I told her that would be just fine with me. It's not as if I ever wanted to be in it in the first place.

Deep down, though, that would be so humiliating. Rejected by the rejects! I can just imagine what Becca would have to say about that. I slump in my seat and stare glumly out the window. Sometimes it's tiring, always having to worry about what Becca Chadwick will think or say. The one good thing about this stupid book club is that I can be myself. Mostly, anyway.

We pull into the parking lot. We were supposed to meet at the Delaneys', but at the last minute Mrs. Hawthorne changed it to the library instead. Neutral territory, I guess. I'm just as glad. I'd rather not share a living room with a bunch of chickens. And I'd just as soon not see another goat as long as I live.

The others are already gathered in the conference room. Mrs. Hawthorne is sitting at the head of the table. Emma is to her right, then Jess, and across from them are Cassidy and her mother. There's no sign of Mr. Delaney.

"Have a seat, Megan," says Mrs. Hawthorne. Her tone is cool.

My mother takes a seat at the far end opposite Mrs. Hawthorne, which means I'm stuck next to Cassidy, facing Jess. Well, facing the top of her head. She's intently inspecting the table, and doesn't look up when I sit down.

"As you can see, I asked the others to arrive a little before you," Emma's mother continues. "We were planning to take a vote and see whether we should allow you to remain in the book club, but we got to talking and decided that a vote would be a little premature. We did come to one conclusion, which I'll get to in a minute, but meanwhile there are some things we feel are only fair to discuss with you directly before voting."

This is all so embarrassing. It's like I'm on trial or something. And Mrs. Hawthorne sounds so serious! I want to tell her to lighten up, for Pete's sake.

"Megan, do you remember chapter 8 in the book?" asks Mrs. Sloane. "The one called 'Jo Meets Apollyon'?"

I can't help it, I take mental notes of her outfit. Black wool pants, gleaming black leather boots, pink sweater (probably cashmere), and a chic silk scarf with a geometric pattern in black, pink, and white. Straight out of *Vogue* magazine.

"Megan?"

"Um, yeah, I guess so. I kind of remember it."

"That's the chapter where Amy burns Jo's manuscript," says Emma helpfully.

"That's right," says Mrs. Sloane.

So what's your point? I want to say, but one glance at my mother's

Heather Vogel Frederick

stony face tells me it's better to keep my mouth shut. Unless I want to be grounded for life.

"Megan, you did to Jess exactly what Amy did to Jo," says Mrs. Hawthorne. "You destroyed something of great value to her."

"I didn't destroy anything!" I say indignantly. "It was just a joke!"

"A cruel and hurtful joke," says Mrs. Hawthorne.

"Kind of like calling someone 'Goat Girl,'" adds Cassidy. "You and the Fab Four are always talking about everybody behind their backs."

"Like you don't," I retort.

"The point is, you destroyed what should have been a happy memory for Jess," Mrs. Hawthorne explains. "Her first opening night, her first big role. And you ruined it."

"Plus, you scared Sundance!" says Emma.

I open my mouth to reply, then close it again. Who cares about a stupid goat? Everyone is looking at me, waiting for me to say something. If they're expecting me to beg for forgiveness or something, they can forget it. No way. It's not my fault that Jess got all upset at a silly practical joke.

My mother's expression is completely blank, which means she's either embarrassed or angry, or both. Probably both.

"It wasn't even my idea," I mumble. "It was Becca's."

Mrs. Hawthorne raises an eyebrow. "Just like it was Becca's idea to read Emma's diary at the ice rink?" she asks. "I was hoping perhaps that incident would have made an impression on you, Megan. Character is about the choices we make in life, and I'm disappointed that you didn't think more carefully about hurting someone else's feelings, or have the courage to stick up for your friend."

Emma's not my friend, I want to tell her, but then I look at Emma and feel a stab of guilt. We were friends once. We used to have a lot of fun together, back then.

"Yeah," says Emma. "How would you like it if someone took your fashion design notebook and showed it to everybody and made fun of it?"

If looks could kill, Emma Hawthorne would be six feet under in Sleepy Hollow Cemetery right now. The happy memories that had tiptoed in for a few seconds go flying right out the window. She has no right to bring that up.

"You still have a fashion design notebook?" my mother says, looking at me in surprise.

"She keeps it in the bottom drawer of her desk," Emma says triumphantly. "Under the paper for her computer printer."

Mrs. Hawthorne sighs. "Girls, girls," she says. "Please. Our book club is in peril here. We're a community, and a community only works if it's based on trust and respect. It's the same with friendship."

"Friendship?" The word bursts out of me unbidden. "What friendship? They're always leaving me out." I look at Emma and Jess and Cassidy accusingly. "You get together and hang out and bake cookies and have sleepovers and I'm never invited."

"You wouldn't have come even if we had invited you!" counters Emma, which is probably true, but still, it's beside the point. "And maybe if you weren't so mean to everybody all the time, you would have been invited."

Something inside me snaps. "You're just jealous!" I yell at her. "Ever since my dad struck it rich and we moved out to Strawberry Hill you've been jealous of me. I see the way you look at my cell phone and my clothes and our cars—but it's not my fault you have to wear Nicole Patterson's hand-me-downs!"

"Megan!" says my mother sharply. "That's enough!"

"But it's true!"

"Look who's talking about being jealous!" Emma yells back. "You were so jealous of Jess's getting the part of Belle in the play that you spread those rumors at school and then tried to sabotage her opening night! She's a better singer than you and you just can't stand it!"

"Now, girls," Mrs. Sloane breaks in. "This isn't productive."

"I guess what we really want to know at this point, Megan, is whether or not you're even interested in remaining a member of the Mother-Daughter Book Club." The gentleness in Mrs. Hawthorne's voice catches me by surprise, and to my horror and shame I burst into tears. The truth is, she's right. I should have stuck up for Emma that day at the rink. Of course I knew better, but I felt trapped and I didn't know what to do. I didn't want Becca and Ashley and Jen to stop liking me. The truth is, I really miss Emma. I miss spending time with her in her pink kitchen, baking cookies and making clothes for our Barbies. I hate myself for being such a coward and I hate it that Emma and Jess and Cassidy shut me out and I hate it that I even care.

"I'll take that as a yes," says Mrs. Hawthorne kindly.

My mother passes me a tissue.

Mrs. Sloane pulls a sheet of paper out of her book club folder and places it on the conference room table in front of me. "Rules of Conduct" is printed across the top. "We want you to sign these," she says.

Mrs. Hawthorne glances around the table. "In fact, I think we all need to sign these. There's no harm in reminding ourselves of the importance of upholding the club rules."

We go over the list together, and under my mother's watchful eye I sign my name at the bottom. I pass the piece of paper to Cassidy and she signs too, then passes it on. When everyone's had a chance to sign, Mrs. Hawthorne turns to me again.

"As I mentioned earlier this evening, the five of us discussed one other thing before you arrived," she told me. "We all agreed that it's only fair that you find a way to make this up somehow to Jess."

I look over at Jess, who hasn't said a single word this entire time. She still won't meet my gaze.

"You can start by apologizing," my mother says firmly, fixing me with the evil-witch-mother eye of death.

"Uh, sorry, Jess," I mumble.

"You can do better than that," my mother prods.

I take a deep breath. "I'm sorry about the stupid practical joke, Jess. Really, truly sorry. I hope you'll forgive me. And I hope your goat is okay, too." For good measure, I look over at Emma. "And I'm sorry

Heather Vogel Frederick

about what happened that day at the ice rink, with your journal."

"That's more like it," says my mother, smiling at me in approval. I smile back.

"I have an idea," says Emma. "About how Megan can make it up to Jess, I mean."

"Go on," says Mrs. Sloane.

"Well, Spring Fling is coming up in a couple of months. The middle school dance. Maybe Megan could design a dress for Jess to wear to it."

"What a wonderful idea!" says Mrs. Hawthorne.

"I'll buy the fabric," my mother announces. I stare at her, shocked. She shrugs and smiles at me again. "It's a worthy cause."

"And you can use my sewing machine," offers Mrs. Sloane.

"I wasn't planning to go to Spring Fling," Jess murmurs, clearly caught off-guard by the whole idea.

"Well, you're going now," says Cassidy. "Is it a deal, Megan?"

I have to admit that designing a real dress sounds like fun. "Yeah, okay."

The door opens and Mr. Delaney comes in carrying a paper bag and a stack of paper plates. Close on his heels is Mrs. Chadwick.

"Am I too early?" he asks, glancing over at me.

Mrs. Hawthorne shakes her head. "Right on time."

"Phoebe, I thought the library board made it clear that you weren't to meet here," Becca's mother says.

Mrs. Hawthorne regards her calmly. "You certainly did make it clear, Calliope. But I checked with the rest of the board, and they have no problem with it. You're outvoted."

Becca's mother looks indignant. She opens her mouth, but before she can say anything Mr. Delaney pulls an apple pie out of the bag and sets it on the table.

"What is *that*?" Mrs. Chadwick cries accusingly.

"An apple pie," Mr. Delaney replies. "Fresh out of the oven. Not nearly as good as the pies Shannon makes, I'm afraid, but perhaps it will do for a cold winter's night."

Mrs. Chadwick turns smugly to Mrs. Hawthorne. "You can't wiggle out of this one," she says. "The library has a strict no-food policy, and you know it. You'll have to remove that pie at once."

"If you stay and help us eat it, then there won't be any food in the library, will there?" says Mrs. Hawthorne mildly.

Becca's mother eyes the pie.

"It looks *enormously* delicious, doesn't it?" says Emma sweetly.

Mrs. Hawthorne looks over at her. The corners of her mouth quirk up. "*Hugely* tasty, I'd say."

"My dad is a *colossally* fabulous cook," adds Jess, the picture of innocence.

Cassidy whispers something to her mother, who grins. I grin too. I haven't played the synonym game since fourth grade.

"Could I please have a *jumbo*-sized piece?" I say.

"Me, too," says Clementine Sloane. "I could eat a *horse*."

"An *elephant*," adds Cassidy. "Maybe even a *mammoth*."

Heather Vogel Frederick

By now we're all grinning broadly. Mrs. Chadwick doesn't notice. She's still focused on the pie.

"Well, just a sliver, I suppose," she says finally.

Mr. Delaney cuts the pie and Mrs. Hawthorne hands the plates and forks around the table. "Here you go, Megs," she says to me.

"Thanks, Mrs. H." It feels good to hear my old nickname, and even better to hear the warmth in Emma's mother's voice. My heart feels lighter than it has for weeks.

My cell phone vibrates in my pocket. It's probably Becca, wanting to know what's going on. I pick up my fork and take a bite of pie and ignore it.

SPRING

"Mothers have need of sharp eyes and discreet tongues when they have girls to manage."

—*Little Women*

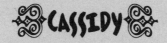

CASSIDY

"Why weren't we all boys, then there wouldn't be any bother . . ."

"COM-ETS! COM-ETS! COM-ETS!"

I can hear them in the stands as I blaze down the ice toward the Minutemen's goal. The Hawthornes, the Wongs, the Delaneys, my sister Courtney, Zach, Ethan, and Dr. Weisman and his wife. Even Becca and Ashley and Jen, though they're mostly here to see the boys, not the game. They're all on their feet, screaming for the team and for me. Only my mother is still in her seat, her hands pressed over her eyes.

She's been like this all night. All season, in fact. Hockey still scares her.

Tonight is the final game of our region's PeeWee Hockey Championships. With two minutes left to go in the third period, the Comets trail the Minutemen by one goal, and we have control of the puck. Correction: I have control of the puck.

With a flick of my wrist I shoot it over to Darcy, our center. Kyle is right wing, and as I make a move toward the goal he swoops in to block a rush by a Minutemen defenseman.

"Go, Cassidy! Go, Darcy!" I hear Mr. Hawthorne holler.

Kyle's block gives me an opening and I take it. Darcy whips the puck back to me and I slice at it for all I'm worth. The crowd erupts with cheers as the goalie lunges, misses, and the puck flies into the net. Score!

A whistle pierces through the noise of the crowd as the Minutemen's coach calls a time-out. We skate over to the Comets bench and grab our water bottles.

Darcy gives me a high five. So does Kyle. Coach Danner slaps the back of my helmet. "Way to go, Sloane!" he crows. "Way to tie it up!"

Coach has long since gotten over the shock of having a girl on his team. Especially since I've been high scorer for most of the season. Darcy says if I keep this up, I have a good shot at MVP.

"A few more plays like that, and we can win this thing," Coach Danner says. His eyes are alight with excitement. "But it's gonna take hustle, it's gonna take drive, and above all it's gonna take the kind of teamwork that just got us that last goal. We can't let our guard down for a second. The Minutemen are going to throw everything they've got at us. They've won the championship the last three years in a row, and they're not going to give it up easily."

I take another gulp of water and look up into the stands. If only Dad were here to see this! Even though he isn't, I'm riding a wave of happiness so big right now that nothing can shake me off it. Not even missing him. My mother, who is sitting up straight and looking out at the rink now that nothing's happening, waves at me. So does Dr. Weisman. I wave my stick back at them jubilantly.

Heather Vogel Frederick

I glance over at the Minutemen's bench. Their coach is standing a little apart, next to his two defensemen. He points at me, and they nod. This strikes me as a little strange, but the whistle blows again and we're back on the ice before I can give it another thought. Darcy and the Minutemen's center face-off, and then the Minutemen have the puck and they're driving toward the goal and all I'm thinking about is the ice and the moves and the missile that is my body. I'm an arrow, a race car, a rocket, crouching low and flying under the radar. The Minutemen's forward feints left, but I'm on him. I snake my stick in and scoop the puck away and the crowd is on its feet again as I spin around and race back toward the goal.

The shouts throb inside my helmet.

"COM-ETS! COM-ETS! COM-ETS!"

It's like déjà vu—I'm blazing down the ice again with the goal in reach. Only this goal is the one that will push us over the top and win us the championship. Nothing can stop me.

I never see it coming.

Next thing I know, I'm flying through the air. I smash into the boards and bounce off like a yo-yo. As I tumble downward, my skates get caught in my stick and my head jerks back and the last thing I hear before my helmet slams against the ice is the ref screaming, "BOARDING!"

Time passes. How much, I don't know. My eyelids flutter open. The bright lights of the arena overhead make me squint. For a moment I have absolutely no idea where I am.

"Is she going to be okay?" I hear my mother ask. Her voice is tight with fear.

"She'll be fine, Mrs. Sloane," I hear Coach Danner reply. "Doc says she's not concussed."

"What happened? I didn't see."

"She got boarded by a Minutemen defenseman."

"What's that?"

"It's an illegal move. He checked her into the boards from behind."

"I thought bodychecking wasn't allowed in PeeWee hockey!"

Coach Danner sighs. "This is twelve-and-up, Mrs. Sloane. Technically, it's allowed now at this age. But not boarding. Don't worry, that player is out for the rest of the game."

"But how—"

"I'm not sure, Mrs. Sloane. He told the ref it was his idea, but it's possible that his coach told him to do it. Cassidy's been high scorer all night, and she was playing brilliantly. It was certainly to their team's advantage to take her out."

I sit up, gingerly touching the lump on the back of my head. My mother bursts into tears.

"It's okay, Mom," I croak. "I'm okay." I look around, wondering how I got to the bench. I turn to Coach Danner. "Is the game over?"

"No, honey," he says. "I called a time-out. We moved you here after Doc checked you over. You weren't out long at all."

Courtney and the entire Mother-Daughter Book Club are leaning over the railing behind the bench watching us.

"Is she okay?" calls Mrs. Hawthorne anxiously.

My mother nods and blows her nose.

Heather Vogel Frederick

"I've never seen anyone move so fast in my entire life," says Mrs. Wong. "I thought you had wings, Clementine!"

Mom laughs shakily. I tug on Coach Danner's jacket. "Coach, right before I went in just then?"

"Yes?"

"I saw the Minutemen's coach say something to those two skaters." I point to the defenseman sulking in the penalty box, and his teammate nearby. "Then he pointed at me."

Coach Danner regards me soberly. "Are you absolutely sure about this, Cassidy?"

"Uh-huh."

My mother's eyes narrow. "Does that mean what I think it means, Bob?"

Coach Danner nods reluctantly. "Looks like it."

My mother rises to her feet. She puts her hands on her hips and glares at the opposing team's coach. "What's his name?"

"Stan Hall."

My mother grabs Coach Danner's bullhorn and holds it up to her mouth. "Coach Stanley Hall, your presence is required at the Comets' bench," she announces. Her voice carries across the arena, the imperious voice of Queen Clementine, and the crowd falls silent. "Immediately," she adds.

With my mother in full supermodel mode, Coach Hall has no choice but to obey. He swaggers over, taking his time.

"What?" he says belligerently.

"Did you tell your players to hurt my daughter?" my mother

demands. The Mother-Daughter Book Club is lined up along the rail behind her, arms folded across chests, scowling.

Coach Hall flicks me a glance. "Of course not," he says.

"I saw you," I tell him.

"Maybe you don't know what you're talking about."

"Maybe she does," my mother snaps. "My daughter doesn't lie."

"Well maybe your precious *daughter* should be practicing pretty little leaps and twirls instead of taking up my team's valuable time," he blusters. "We've got a championship match to finish here, in case you didn't notice. It's not my fault hockey's a rough game. The rink is no place for a princess."

"Is that so?" says my mother. She's a full head taller than Coach Hall, and she stares down at him, unblinking. His gaze falters after a few seconds, and he looks away. My mother continues, "It seems to me that my 'princess,' as you put it, has been wiping the ice all night with those PeeWee peabrains of yours out there."

Coach Danner is watching my mother, fascinated. Queen Clementine has that effect on people.

"A bit of a coincidence that the game's high scorer is suddenly down and out," she adds. "Don't you think?" Her voice drops to a whisper. "If I ever catch you pulling a trick like that again, I'll wipe the ice with you myself."

She turns away. The royal audience is over, and Coach Hall is dismissed. He stands there uncomfortably for a moment, looks over at the Mother-Daughter Book Club—who are all smiling broadly now—clears his throat, and retreats to the Minutemen bench. His swagger has vanished, I note with satisfaction.

Heather Vogel Frederick

"I can see where Cassidy gets her spirit," says Coach Danner, looking at my mother admiringly.

"Way to go, Mom," I tell her.

She smiles at me, and then her regal composure vanishes and her face crumples and she hugs me to her fiercely. "Oh, sweetheart, for a moment I thought—"

"It's okay, Mom, really," I assure her. "I'm fine." I glance up to where Dr. Weisman is sitting in the stands. I know exactly what my mother thought.

She looks over at Coach Danner. "Is she really fine?"

"Absolutely. But I'll keep her out for the rest of the game just to be sure, if you'd like."

My mother's arms tighten around me. I stiffen. "I'm fine," I tell her, pushing away. "Please, Mom."

She looks at me searchingly.

"Mom," I ask, struck with sudden inspiration. "What would Jo March do?"

My mother's mouth drops open. "Cassidy Ann Sloane!" she cries in disbelief. "I can't believe you're quoting *Little Women!*" She glances up at Mrs. Wong and Mrs. Hawthorne. "Did you hear that? My baby is quoting Louisa May Alcott!"

"You go, girl!" calls Emma's mother. Everybody else grins and gives me a thumbs-up.

"For Pete's sake," I mumble, embarrassed.

My mother looks down at me and smiles. "Maybe there's hope for you after all," she says. Then she looks over at the penalty box and the smile vanishes. "I'll tell you what Jo March would do. Jo March would get right back out there and kick some Minutemen you-know-what. And she'd be right. I think it's time to show Coach Hall what this princess is really made of."

I throw my arms around her. "Thanks!"

"Your dad would be so proud of you," she whispers into my hair. "I know I am."

I put my helmet back on and get some quick last-minute advice from Coach Danner and then I skate back out onto the ice. The crowd gives me a standing ovation.

The ref gives me the puck, blows the whistle, and we're back in the game with thirty seconds to go.

I whip the puck over to Kyle, who passes it to Darcy while I deke to the left and skip by the Minutemen's right wing. I zoom past Coach Hall. His face looks like thunder, but there's nothing he can do to stop me now. Darcy passes and I catch the puck and drive toward the goal.

The crowd is screaming for me now. "CASS-I-DY! CASS-I-DY! CASS-I-DY!"

I smile as I lift the puck, catching it right in the sweet spot on the blade of my stick, just like Dad taught me. I glance up at the stands. My mother is on her feet with the rest of the Mother-Daughter Book Club, and her eyes are wide open this time. She's watching me. She's not afraid anymore.

And as I snap the puck and watch it soar straight into the Minutemen's goal, my jubilant heart soars right along with it.

Heather Vogel Frederick

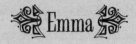

Emma

"Boys are trying enough to human patience,
goodness knows! but girls are infinitely more so."

"Emma! Wake up! It's time!"

I crack open one eyelid and freeze. For a split second I think I'm dreaming. There's a soldier standing at the foot of my bed. He's wearing a uniform and carrying a musket and everything. Then I recognize him: He's a minuteman. He's my father. It's April nineteenth.

My father flips on the light and strikes a pose. "The Concord Hymn, by Ralph Waldo Emerson," he announces. I let out a groan but he ignores me and begins to recite.

> *"By the rude bridge that arched the flood,*
> *Their flag to April's breeze unfurled,*
> *Here once the embattled farmers stood*
> *And fired the shot heard round the world."*

I throw my pillow at him, knocking his tricorn hat off. He laughs, bends down and picks it up, then leaves, shutting the door behind him.

Patriot's Day is a big deal here in Concord. It's a school holiday, and there's a big parade, and lots of crazy people including my parents drag their kids out of bed at the crack of dawn to go to the Old North Bridge for the battle reenactment. "It's educational!" my mother always says, which is mom-code for "It's guaranteed to bore you to tears but you're going anyway because it's good for you." "It's a time-honored family tradition," my dad insists whenever Darcy and I protest.

Already, minutemen are gathering in neighboring towns, ready to re-create the march to the Old North Bridge, where over two centuries ago the patriots faced off against the British in the skirmish that sparked the Revolutionary War. People get all excited about the battle reenactment, but it's mostly just a bunch of musket fire and soldiers on both sides falling down pretending to be dead. It's kind of fun, though. And afterward, everyone sticks around for a big pancake breakfast.

Shivering, I reach for my glasses and crawl out of bed, nearly tripping over Cassidy. She mumbles something and rolls over, sliding off the air mattress onto the floor. "Huh?" she says, sitting up and rubbing her eyes.

"Time to get up!"

Jess, who won the coin toss for the top bunk, buries her head under her pillow. "You've got to be kidding," she whines in a muffled voice.

Heather Vogel Frederick

I whip it off heartlessly. "C'mon, Princess Ramshackle. We're leaving soon. You don't want to miss all the fun."

"You Hawthornes are crazy," says Megan, from the other air mattress on the floor. She burrows down into her sleeping bag.

"Totally nuts," I agree, grabbing the foot of the bag and dragging it off the mattress. She lands on the floor with a thud.

It's our first annual Mother-Daughter Book Club Patriot's Day sleepover. Mom suggested it, since Jess always stays over anyway. Her father and my dad are both volunteer minutemen. Mom thought it would be a good way to introduce Cassidy to a bit of Concord's history. Having Megan here too feels good, like a puzzle whose pieces were scattered that has been put back together again. Not perfectly— Megan's piece still has some jagged edges—but still, it's a whole puzzle again.

Megan's been pretty quiet since the emergency book club meeting. As far as I can tell, the Fab Four are still thick as thieves, as Mom puts it, but Megan's being a lot nicer these days, and Jess and Cassidy and I are careful to include her more in the stuff we do. Like this sleepover, for instance.

Not that it was much of a sleepover. We couldn't stay up late because the reenactment starts at dawn, and my parents wouldn't let us watch the movie about the Revolutionary War that Darcy and Kyle rented. Too gory, they said. So after we made cookies we mostly just hung out here in my room, where we talked about school and Cassidy entertained us by burping the alphabet. She made us laugh so hard my mom came in and threatened to separate us if we didn't settle down and get to sleep. Which we finally did.

"Five minutes!" my dad calls from downstairs, and we scramble for the sweats and fleece we laid out last night. It's still cold out this time of year, especially this early in the morning.

"I look like a rooster," says Megan glumly, inspecting herself in the mirror. She takes a comb and tackles the offending bed-head hair. "I just hope we don't run into any boys."

I don't say anything. Zach Norton is one topic that Megan and I don't discuss. At all. Ever.

We troop down to the kitchen, where my mother has orange juice waiting for us. It's way too early to eat anything. Getting up at four A.M. always makes me feel a little queasy.

"Woo-hoo!" crows Cassidy, catching sight of the knee breeches Darcy and Kyle are wearing. "Where's the rest of your pants, guys?"

This is Darcy's first year as a minuteman. Kyle's, too. You have to be in eighth grade to join the reenactment militia. My brother has been looking forward to this forever. Dad bought him the knee breeches, the vest—the whole outfit. He says this is the father-son version of our book club.

"Shut up, Sloane," Darcy replies good-naturedly. He takes off his tricorn hat and jams it on her head, which is a mass of fiery red tangles as usual. Cassidy always looks like she has bed-head. "You're in Concord now, not California," he tells her. "Breeches are what true patriots wear, right, Kyle?"

Heather Vogel Frederick

Kyle nods. "Think of them as historical surf shorts."

Cassidy laughs.

Jess regards my brother shyly. "I think you look nice," she says.

"Thanks, Jess." Darcy plucks his hat back from Cassidy. "See, Sloane? Some people have manners."

Megan doesn't say anything, but I can tell from the way she's looking at my brother that she thinks he looks nice too. It's weird to think that my friends might actually like my brother. As in boyfriend, I mean.

"So, is everyone clear on the plan?" says my dad.

We all nod. While they head off to join their regiment, we'll meet up with the Wongs and Cassidy's mom and sister. Jess's dad will leave the twins with us once he gets there, and afterward, we'll all rendezvous at the pancake breakfast and then come back here to our house for the parade. We're right on the parade route, and the best spot to see it is from our front yard. Or from the branches of our big oak tree. Darcy and I usually climb the tree.

"Let's go, girls!" says my mother, and we stumble groggily down Lowell Road toward Minuteman National Park. We stake out a good spot on Buttrick Hill overlooking the Old North Bridge and wait. As the sky begins to lighten, the crowd grows, and with it the sense of anticipation. In the distance I hear the rattle of drums and the sharp, piercing marches of the fifes. The music grows closer, announcing the arrival of regiments from Lexington and Maynard and Acton and Boxboro, all the neighboring towns. Just like they did over two hundred years ago, the minutemen are gathering, alerted to the movement of the British troops by Paul Revere and Samuel Prescott. Well, actors pretending to be Paul Revere and Samuel Prescott.

I spot lots of kids from school. Ethan is here with his dad and his older brother, and I see the Pattersons from church. For once, I'm not wearing anything of Nicole's. There's no sign of Zach Norton or the rest of the Fab Four yet, though Becca, at least, will probably turn up. Her brother Stewart is in the reenactment for the first time this year, just like Darcy and Kyle. He's not a minuteman, though. The Chadwicks have always played the part of British soldiers because their ancestors were Tories. I'm glad my dad and Darcy don't have to be redcoats.

"There's my father," Jess shouts, and we all wave wildly at him. Mr. Delaney spots us and threads his way through the crowd, dragging a pair of sleepy, protesting twins.

"Almost didn't make it," he tells my mother. "These two are a handful."

"We'll take it from here," says my mother, plucking them skillfully away from him.

"Thanks," he replies gratefully, and trots over to join his regiment.

"When I get bigger I'm going to be a minuteman too," brags Dylan, staring after his father.

"Me, too," says Ryan.

"Nuh-uh," says Dylan. "I said minuteman first. You have to be a redcoat."

Heather Vogel Frederick

"No way," Ryan retorts. "They were the bad guys."

"You have to be a red-coat! You have to be a red-coat!" Dylan chants gleefully. Ryan flies at him, enraged, and the two of them tumble onto the wet grass, where they scuffle like puppies.

"Will you boys quit it!" scolds Jess.

"Who wants cocoa?" cries my mother, whipping a thermos out of her bag and holding up some paper cups. This gets the twins' attention, and their argument is instantly forgotten as they crowd around her for the treat.

"Little brothers are a pain in the neck," grumbles Jess.

Megan looks at them wistfully. "I think they're kind of cute," she says. "I wouldn't mind having a little brother."

Jess snorts. "You're welcome to one of mine anytime."

Mrs. Sloane and Courtney arrive, yawning, along with the Wongs. Mrs. Wong is carrying a cardboard container lined with coffee cups. "Soy lattes," she says, handing them to the grownups. "A healthy wake-me-up."

Megan waves to Becca, who is standing with her mother alongside the families of the men playing British soldiers. Their crowd seems a little subdued, and keeps apart from the rest of us, which of course is silly since we're all Americans now. Still, like I said before, I'm glad Dad and Darcy get to be patriots.

"Samuel Prescott!" someone shouts, and the crowd surges forward, straining for a glimpse of the man on horseback. Sure enough, on the far side of the bridge a black horse appears. It thunders across the wooden slats spanning the river and comes to a halt. The rider faces the gathered soldiers and shouts out the traditional warning: "The British are coming!"

The crowd takes up the cry as the minutemen all take their places.

I shiver, as much with cold as with excitement for the coming battle. At least it's not raining. Or worse, sleeting. One year we even had snow. Family tradition or no family tradition, there's nothing worse than standing in a soggy field at five in the morning, shivering under an umbrella.

A flash of scarlet across the river signals the arrival of the redcoats. A musket cracks and I flinch. The battle has begun.

"Cool!" says Cassidy, watching the action unfold in front of us. As the patriots and redcoats fire on one another, smoke from the muskets drifts across the field like mist. A minuteman falls, and then another. A British soldier, too. I think it's Mr. Chadwick.

A few minutes later, it's finished. The fallen dead stand up again and brush themselves off, and the troops shake hands, then line up for the twenty-one-gun salute. I like this part of the ceremony best. As the cannon booms out again and again across the meadows, I close my eyes, feeling its thunder echo in my bones and in the hollow of my chest.

"Would you girls watch the twins for a few minutes?" my mother asks. "There's someone here I'd like Clementine to meet."

She hands Dylan and Ryan off to us and drifts away with Mrs. Sloane and the Wongs. Cassidy watches her go, a funny expression on her face. Last night she told us that she thinks maybe her mother has a boyfriend. I guess Mrs. Sloane has been spending a lot more time than usual checking her e-mail, and once or twice Cassidy and her sister have seen the name "Fred" in the return address field. She gets packages and mail from him all the time now too. Cassidy is not thrilled with this idea at all, of course. I wouldn't be either.

As we line up for pancakes and sausages, Jess's little brothers are afire with excitement and it's all we can do to hang onto them. The hot food tastes good, and we tuck in hungrily. All around us, minutemen and redcoats alike do the same, mingling cheerfully as they eat.

Well, mostly cheerfully.

"Lobsterback!" I hear Dylan cry.

"Rotten redcoat!" Ryan adds.

We turn around to see that the twins have armed themselves with sticks, which they're jabbing at Stewart Chadwick, who's trying to eat his breakfast. Dylan's makeshift bayonet accidentally hits the plate, and the pancakes go flying.

Becca grabs Dylan's arm and shakes him. Hard. He cries out and Jess whips around.

"Hey!" she calls. "Leave my brother alone!"

Becca's eyes narrow as she looks from one to the other. "He's your brother, is he? I should have known by his manners." She smirks at Dylan. "Raised in a barn just like your sister, were you, Goat Boy?"

Jess's face flushes with anger. She marches over to Becca. "His name isn't Goat Boy, it's Dylan," she snaps. "Let go of his arm."

Cassidy and I exchange a glance. What's gotten into shy Jess?

"Who's going to make me?" Becca demands. "You?" She gives Dylan another shake. "Little beast shouldn't be running around without a leash."

Cassidy and I hurry over to stand beside Jess. Ashley and Jen drift over next to Becca, looking a little sheepish. As well they should—they both have pesty little brothers of their own. Megan walks over too, but she doesn't join either group. Instead, she stands apart slightly. "Let him go, Becca," she says.

Becca lifts an eyebrow. "I should have known you'd side with your little book club friends," she sneers. "Traitor." She glances over at Ashley and Jen. "It's us or them. Right, girls?"

Ashley and Jen snicker nervously. They look over at Megan, then at Becca. Finally, they shrug and nod. "Stupid wannabees," I mutter to Cassidy.

"Buzz, buzz, buzz," she mutters back.

We all stand there glaring at each other, the Mother-Daughter Book Club versus the Fab Four. Or possibly Fab Three. Something is hanging in the balance here, something important. A line has been drawn in the sand. It's like we're fighting our own private war of sorts, right here on this historical battlefield. I hold my breath, wondering what Megan will do.

She doesn't even hesitate. Glancing over at me, she smiles a real honest-to-goodness Megan smile. Then she calmly plops her plate of pancakes right on top of Becca Chadwick's head.

"Aaauugh!" cries Becca, dropping Dylan's arm as her hands fly up to her syrup-covered hair.

"Way to go, Wong!" says Cassidy in astonished admiration.

Heather Vogel Frederick

I am speechless. So is Jess. Dylan runs over to her, and she puts her arms around him protectively.

"You *creep*!" screams Becca. "What did you do that for?"

"Pick on someone your own size next time," says Megan.

"You'd better believe I will!" Becca grabs Ashley's paper plate and throws it at Megan.

Megan ducks and the pancakes hit Cassidy instead, who launches herself at the Fab Three with a howl of rage. In a flash, pancakes and sausages are flying everywhere. The crowd quickly moves away from us as Ryan and Dylan get in on the act too.

I look up from mashing my plate against the side of Jen Webster's face to see Mrs. Chadwick bearing down on us. She grabs a twin in each meaty hand. "Where are your parents?" she demands.

"The boys are with me," says my mother, who is right on her heels. She unhooks the twins from Mrs. Chadwick's grasp. "And so are these four wildcats. The battle's over, girls."

Becca's mother puts her hands on her ample hips. "Who started this?" she demands.

Becca points to Megan. "She did!"

"It's the influence of that terrible club," Mrs. Chadwick says. "I knew it!"

"Megan didn't start it, Becca did," says Jess. "She hurt my brother."

Mrs. Chadwick swells up at this accusation. "It's hardly my daughter's fault that your beastly little brother is so out-of-control," she says. "Now, if your mother were here—"

"That's enough, Calliope." My mother's voice is sharp.

"Well," she huffs. "All I'm saying is you should keep them under better control." She trundles off, dabbing at Becca's sticky hair with a napkin. Ashley and Jen slink after them.

My mother, Mrs. Sloane, and Mrs. Wong turn and stare at the four of us silently. I can barely see through the bits of pancake squished into my glasses, and I can feel syrup dripping down the back of my neck. Cassidy fishes a piece of sausage out from behind her ear, inspects it, then pops it into her mouth. Her mother closes her eyes and shakes her head. Her shoulders start to twitch. I relax a little. She's laughing.

"They had it coming, Mom," I tell my mother.

She gives me a rueful smile. "I don't doubt it," she replies. "Well, whoever started it, it doesn't matter now. What matters is that we get you girls cleaned up before the parade starts."

Trailing bits of breakfast, we head toward home. At the top of Buttrick Hill we pass the Concord militia, who are gathered under a stand of elms. We all wave to Dad and Darcy and Mr. Delaney. Their mouths drop open when they see us.

"Don't even ask," my mother tells them.

"Hey, look! There's Third!" cries Cassidy.

Sure enough, Third and his father (do they call him Second, since he's Cranfield Bartlett II?) are there with the others. Technically, Third is too young to be a minuteman, but he's been playing the drums since he was in a playpen, practically, and he's really good, so they made an

Heather Vogel Frederick

exception. He's the regiment's drummer boy. He sees us and rattles out a quick beat on his snare drum, showing off.

"Hey, Beauty," says a familiar voice behind me. I turn around to see Zach Norton, and feel a stab of envy when I realize he's talking to Jess.

"Hey, Beast," she replies, smiling shyly.

He picks a piece of pancake out of her hair. "I saw the food fight," he says. "Way to stick up for your brother."

Does Zach really think Jess is beautiful, I wonder, *or is he just saying that because of the play?*

He turns to Cassidy. "So what do you think, Sloane? You have anything like this back in Laguna Beach?"

Cassidy snorts. "Food fights? We'd leave you in the dust."

"I mean the battle, you dork."

Cassidy shakes her head. "Historical in California means, like, anything more than two weeks old," she replies. "I never even heard of the Revolutionary War before we moved here."

Zach doesn't say anything to Megan or me.

Third rattles out another drum tattoo, and the militia throw their paper plates and cups in the trash and fall in line. As the ranks of men head off toward downtown Concord, where they'll assemble for the parade, the fife and drum corps start to play "Yankee Doodle."

"Stuck a pancake on her head and called it macaroni!" sings Cassidy at the top of her lungs, falling in behind them. She turns and grins at us.

Megan and Jess and I grin back. We hurry to join her, and the four of us link arms like victorious soldiers and march off toward home.

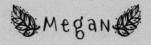

Megan

*"The best of us have a spice of perversity in us,
especially when we are young and in love."*

Emma and I are standing side by side in front of the bathroom mirror. "You look ridiculous," I tell her.

She sticks her tongue out at me. "Look who's talking," she says, and we both burst out laughing.

Back in the kitchen, the Mother-Daughter Book Club is assembled in the Sloanes' breakfast nook. Everyone's hair is pulled back with terrycloth headbands, and all of our faces are bright green. All but my mother's. She's the one holdout, naturally. Tonight is the Spring Fling dance, and Cassidy's mom is giving us all facials with something called Madame Miracle's Mint Mud Mask. Mrs. Sloane is trying to convince my mother to try it.

"See?" she says, pointing to the ingredients. "It says right here: all-natural."

"Shannon sent it from New York," Mrs. Hawthorne points out. "She said it's really popular with the cast of *HeartBeats*."

Mrs. Delaney heard about the "beauty party," as Mrs. Sloane calls it, and sent a whole bunch of makeup and stuff for us to try.

Jess squints at the small print on the tube and reads off the ingredients. "Mrs. Sloane is right," she tells my mother. "They're all herbal."

"I've seen it on the shelf at Nature's Corner," coaxes Mrs. Sloane.

Nature's Corner is the organic grocery where my mother does most of our shopping. When she's not buying things from Half Moon Farm, that is.

"Really?" says my mother. She sniffs the tube suspiciously.

"Smells nice, doesn't it?" says Mrs. Sloane.

"I guess so," my mother concedes. She grudgingly allows her face to be smeared with some of the green goop. "But I'll bet Marmee never did anything like this."

"I don't think they had Madame Miracle back in the Marches' day," says Mrs. Hawthorne.

"If they did, Amy would have liked it," says Emma, giving me a sly look.

"So would Meg," I retort.

"Jo would have hated it," says Cassidy, her green mask set in a scowl. We had to practically hold her down when it was her turn.

"There," says Mrs. Sloane. "Done. Now we just need to let it stay on for half an hour. To work its mint miracle."

She goes to the kitchen sink and washes her hands, then calls upstairs, "Nail polish time!"

Courtney comes clattering down. She opens her eyes wide in mock alarm. "The Martians have landed!"

Her mother holds up her hands and wiggles her fingers. "Yes, and it's time for us aliens to get our nails done," she says.

Courtney pulls out a stool from the kitchen island counter with a flourish. "Moms first," she orders. "I'll start with Mrs. Wong, then you're next, Mrs. Hawthorne."

"Age before beauty, eh, Lily?" says Mrs. Hawthorne.

"Speak for yourself," my mother retorts. "I'm sure this mask is peeling years off my face."

They both giggle.

The Sloanes' kitchen is huge, nearly as big as ours. It's cozier than our ultramodern one on Strawberry Hill, though. Our kitchen is all stark stainless steel and granite. The Sloanes' is more homey, with blue gingham curtains and a panel of stained-glass windows in the breakfast nook that's making pretty patterns of yellow and blue and green on the white farmhouse table.

"Who makes up these names?" asks Mrs. Hawthorne, squinting at the labels on the jars of nail polish from Mrs. Delaney. "Listen to this. 'Siren Song.' 'Apple-icious.' 'Tickled Pink.'" She shakes her head. "Somebody, somewhere, is getting paid to come up with these ridiculous things."

"Really?" says Emma. "I want that job."

"No, you don't, darling, you're much too smart." Mrs. Hawthorne looks at our green faces. "You're all much too smart, even if maybe you don't look it right at this moment."

I smile, and I can feel my mud mask crack. A few minutes later the

Heather Vogel Frederick

buzzer goes off and Mrs. Sloane lines us up at the kitchen sink, where she scrubs off our masks with a wet washcloth. Then she slathers on moisturizer that smells like watermelon, and starts in on fixing our hair.

"Jess, there's a note at the bottom of the box from your mom," Mrs. Hawthorne calls from the manicure station. "Why don't you read it to us while we're being bee-yoo-ti-fied?"

"Okay," says Jess. Things haven't been the same with her since Patriot's Day either. Emma says Jess finally found her voice. That's a good way to put it, I guess. Anyway, she's not nearly as shy as she was when we started the book club last fall.

She opens the envelope. "'Dear fans of Little Women,'" she reads. "'A few goodies are enclosed to make my already gorgeous daughter and her gorgeous friends even more stunning.'" Jess looks up and smiles at us. "'Wish I could be there for your debut ball, but *HeartBeats* is going on location to Paris for a week, imagine that! It's honeymoon time for Judd Chance and Larissa LaRue. By the way, I've got the whole cast reading *Little Women* and we love it. We all cried when we got to the part where Beth dies.'"

Jess looks up. "I cried too," she admits.

Mrs. Sloane holds up her hand. "Guilty as charged."

"Ditto," says Emma, and pretty soon we all have our hands up except Cassidy, who says it was stupid and mean of the author to kill off one of her main characters.

"I think I detected a tear or two, when we got to that part," counters her mother in a stage whisper.

I guess they're still reading the book aloud together. I thought that was dumb and babyish when I first heard about it, but now I think that I wouldn't mind, if my mother wanted to.

"Does she say anything else in the note?" asks Mrs. Hawthorne.

"Nope," says Jess. "Just au revoir and oodles of love."

I drift over to the manicure station. "Mom, couldn't you have picked something more exciting than that?" I ask, disappointed to see that she has chosen a boring beige called "Sand Dune."

"I wanted something natural-looking," my mother says.

"Naturally," I reply with a sigh.

When it's my turn, I decide to go with blue, to match my dress. I help Jess pick out a shade of raspberry to match hers, and try convincing Cassidy to give "Gather Ye Rosebuds" a whirl ("No way," she says, and won't budge this time after giving in on the facial). Then I ask Emma what color her dress is.

"Yellow," she says.

"You should try this one, then," I say, handing her a soft lavender. "Purple and yellow are complementary colors. It'll look great."

Emma peers at the bottle. She shudders. "'Shrinking Violet'? Who'd want to wear something called that?"

"So what? The color is perfect."

"Words are important to me," she says stubbornly. "I'm a poet, remember?"

We look at each other and suddenly we both freeze. We've never talked about what happened at the ice rink last winter, never mentioned

"Zach Attack." Fortunately, the back door opens just then and Mr. Hawthorne and Mr. Delaney and my dad come in with Chinese take-out, and the awkward moment is smoothed over in the general rush for food.

Afterward, the four of us go upstairs to get changed.

Nobody has seen Jess's dress or mine. I made them here at Cassidy's house, using Mrs. Sloane's sewing machine just like she promised. She gave me some pointers on design details, and let me look through all her fashion magazines. She has tons of them. And she gave me some leftover ice-blue fabric for my dress.

I designed Jess's dress to look like the prettiest cupcake in the bakery, all frothy pink and scallops and poufed sleeves. My slim sheath is more sophisticated. The dresses are different, but they're both really pretty. At least I think so.

Jess and I are the first ones down. I can't wait to see what everyone thinks. "Ta-da!" I cry, as we float into the kitchen. Well, as Jess and I float. Cassidy clomps. She's wearing one of Courtney's old dresses. It's white, with tiny little roses all over it. Cassidy hates it, of course.

"Wow!" says Mrs. Sloane. "You girls look amazing!"

"You did a fabulous job with Jess's dress," says Mrs. Hawthorne. "Yours, too."

"Thanks, Mrs. H," I reply modestly.

"No kidding," says Courtney, fingering the fabric of my sheath. "I'd pay good money for either one."

"Really?" I reply.

"Absolutely. Do you think you could design something for me for junior prom?"

I look over at my mother. She shrugs, then nods. "Okay, I guess," she says, but there's little enthusiasm in her voice. My happiness deflates a little. My mother is still hoping I'll turn into Super Megan and go to Colonial Academy and MIT and Harvard, but I think she's beginning to realize it's a lost cause. At least she's shut up about that stupid science-and-math camp. Still, I wish she could be proud of me for who I am, instead of worrying about who I'm not.

"Don't you girls look glamorous!" Mr. Hawthorne exclaims, snapping a picture.

"Not yet!" Mrs. Sloane protests. "I haven't finished everyone's makeup! I've only gotten to Emma so far."

"Speaking of my darling daughter, where is she?" asks Mrs. Hawthorne, glancing at her watch. "You girls don't want to be late."

"She's still getting changed," I tell her.

"Makeup?" says Mr. Delaney, rummaging through the box from Jess's mom with a worried expression. "Don't you think the natural look is best for girls their age?"

"Absolutely," agrees my mother, of course.

"Oh, a little blush and mascara never hurt anybody," says Cassidy's mother, waving their concerns away with a flick of her supermodel hand. A hand whose nails are now sporting a particularly scrumptious shade of red called "Hello, Gorgeous!"

Mr. Delaney plucks out a small cylinder and his forehead puckers anxiously. "You're not planning on letting them wear lipstick, though, right?"

"It's just gloss, Dad," says Jess, twirling happily.

Mrs. Hawthorne watches her. Then she looks over at me and Cassidy. She cocks her head and studies our hems, which are just above our knees. She frowns. "Isn't this a formal dance?" she asks.

"No, Phoebe," says my mother. "Didn't you get the flyer from school?"

"If it came, I didn't notice," Mrs. Hawthorne says. "I've been swamped at work. I'm tussling with Calliope and the library board over moving the teen section out of the children's room." She sighs. "Oh, dear, Emma is not going to be happy."

The door opens and Emma walks in. She's wearing a floor-length yellow gown with cap sleeves and a scoop neck with embroidery around it. I recognize it instantly. Nicole Patterson wore it last summer when she was a bridesmaid in her cousin's wedding. Emma stares at Cassidy and Jess and me, stricken.

"My dress is all wrong!" she wails. "Mom, you said this was a formal!"

A guilty look creeps across Mrs. Hawthorne's face. "Oh, honey, I'm so sorry. I guess I was mistaken. But you look beautiful—honest! Doesn't she, girls?"

We cluster around to reassure her.

"You look fine," Cassidy tells her. "Who cares, anyway?"

"I care!" wails Emma again. "I'm not going!"

"Don't be silly," says Mrs. Hawthorne. "You're not going to let a little thing like this stop you."

"It's not a little thing!" cries Emma. "It's a big thing! It's my first middle school dance, and I wanted everything to be perfect! And instead I'm stuck wearing one of Nicole Patterson's hand-me-downs again and it's all wrong and I'm going to be the laughingstock of the whole school!" She bursts into tears. "I hate being poor!"

"Give it to me," I tell her.

"What?"

I hold out my hand. "Your dress. Give it to me."

"Why?" she sniffles.

"I'll fix it for you, nitwit. But I need you to take it off."

Emma's nose is running and so is her mascara. She looks like a raccoon. "Really?" she hiccups. "Do you think you can?"

I nod.

"We don't have much time," warns Mrs. Sloane.

Emma ducks into the pantry and shrugs off the dress. I leave her standing there in her slip and race upstairs to the makeshift sewing room. Emma is the same height as me. I still have the measurements for my dress pinned to the bulletin board, and I check them carefully and measure even more carefully, then I take the scissors and trim off the bottom half of the dress. I only hope this works—if it doesn't, Mrs. Hawthorne will kill me. Not to mention Emma.

I turn on the sewing machine and sew up the hem, add a ruffle of

Heather Vogel Frederick

lace around the bottom, then race back downstairs. "Try this," I say, thrusting the finished product into the pantry. "But you're going to have to ditch the slip."

Emma emerges a moment later. "How do I look?" she asks.

"Perfect," says Mrs. Sloane, beaming. "Absolutely perfect."

"Problem solved," I say smugly.

"Megan, you're a wonder," says Mrs. Hawthorne in admiration. She sees my mother frowning at Emma's remodeled dress. "Lily, did you know that when Louisa May Alcott was twelve, she started her own business?"

"Really?" says my mother.

Mrs. Hawthorne nods. "Yup. She set up shop as a doll's dressmaker. Hung a sign out, put little mannequins in the window and everything. The other children in her neighborhood paid her to sew clothes for their dolls."

"You're making this up!"

"I am not."

My mother looks at Jess's dress. Then she looks at mine. *Really* looks at them this time. "They are quite pretty," she admits cautiously.

I throw my arms around her. She looks surprised, but she hugs me back.

"See?" says Mrs. Sloane. "Fashion isn't so bad after all. It makes lots of people happy."

"It's time to go," says Mrs. Hawthorne, pointing to the clock.

We all kiss our dads good-bye—all of us except Cassidy, that is, who kisses Courtney instead—and pile into the Sloanes' van with our mothers.

"Have fun!" says Mrs. Sloane, letting us off at the gymnasium door.

"Call us on Megan's cell phone when you're ready to be picked up!" adds Mrs. Hawthorne.

"You all look wonderful!" says my mother, and blows me a kiss.

Feeling self-conscious in our finery and high heels, we teeter into the gym. All except Cassidy, who switched into sneakers in the car when her mother wasn't looking. She's as giddy as the rest of us, though. Even Jess, who wasn't so sure she wanted to go, is all wound up. Our first dance! Almost everyone we know will be here. Unfortunately, that includes Becca and Ashley and Jen. Things have been really uncomfortable since our Patriot's Day showdown. Becca has been busy saying all sorts of mean things about me behind my back, of course. I cringe now when I remember how I used to do that too. Cassidy says Becca is a moron and anybody with half a brain knows that so who cares what she says? She's got a point.

Inside the gym, the music is blasting. There's a DJ on the stage, and one of those shiny ball things hanging from the ceiling. I spot Zach across the room with Ethan and Third. The boys see us, too, but make no move to come over and ask us to dance.

"Well, if it isn't the Mother-Daughter Book Club."

We all turn around. It's Becca Chadwick, of course. She's wearing a Kissin' Kate design. I saw it last time I was at the mall. She eyes my dress. "Didn't I see that in the window at Miranda's Garden?" she asks

Heather Vogel Frederick

me with a superior smile. Miranda's Garden is the thrift store where Emma and her mother get most of their clothes.

Becca's trying to insult me, as usual. Or as Emma would say, the queen bee is using her stinger.

"It's *couture*," says Cassidy, putting her hand on her hip and striking a pose worthy of a supermodel's daughter. "Exclusive label and one-of-a-kind. Very expensive. My mom knows the designer."

That shuts Becca up. Ashley and Jen look at me, impressed. "Wow, Megan," says Ashley. "That's awesome!"

"Big deal," mumbles Becca.

Cassidy points to Jess. "The same designer made Jess's dress too."

Becca looks Jess up and down. "Goat Girl in a dress, imagine that," she says. She leans in and sniffs loudly. "Can't get away from the barn-yard, though, can you?"

I watch Jess's face fall. The happiness that had radiated from her at the Sloanes' drains away, and a hot bubble of indignation wells up inside of me and bursts. "If there's anyone who stinks around here, it's you, Becca," I snap.

She waves her hand at me dismissively. "Whatever," she says. "Come on, girls." As she turns to walk away, Ashley and Jen hesitate. They look at me, confused. Then they shrug and drift off after Becca. I watch them go, wondering how on earth I ever thought they were my friends.

"Buzz, buzz, buzz!" says Cassidy. "I hope they sting each other to death."

Zach sneaks up behind her and clamps his hands over her eyes.

"Knock it off, Norton," she says, slapping his hands away.

He laughs. "Never thought I'd see you in a dress."

She glowers at him, and at Ethan and Third, who are hovering a few feet away looking uncomfortable in their slacks and polo shirts. "Take a picture, why don't you!" she says. "It'll last longer!"

The boys laugh, and she picks up the hem of her dress and chases Ethan and Third off toward the refreshment table. The rest of us stand there awkwardly for a moment. Then Zach turns to Jess.

"Would you care to dance, m'lady?" he asks, using the same formal bow he did when he was Beast in the play last winter.

In reply, Jess curtsies. As Zach leads her out onto the dance floor, she casts a troubled glance over his shoulder at Emma. Cassidy returns just in time to see Emma run out of the gym.

"What's wrong with her?" she mumbles, her mouth full of cake.

"I guess we'd better find out."

We snake our way through the knots of dancers and emerge in the middle school's main hallway.

"There she goes!" says Cassidy, pointing to a flash of yellow dissappearing into the girls' room.

We hurry after her. Inside, there's no sign of Emma, but one of the stall doors is closed. Cassidy knocks on it. "Em, are you in there?"

"Go away," says Emma.

"C'mon, Emma, what's the matter?" I ask her, even though I think I already know the answer.

Heather Vogel Frederick

"You wouldn't understand," she says.

"Try me."

The door opens and a raccoon eye peers out. Emma's tears have smudged her mascara again. "How could she?" she whispers. "She knows I like him!"

So do I, I want to say, but don't. This is not the time for true confessions.

Cassidy reaches in and hauls Emma out of the stall. She marches her over to the sink, wets some paper towels, and pats her face with them. "This is stupid," she tells Emma. "It's just Zach you're talking about, not some movie star. So what if he's dancing with Jess?"

This makes Emma wail harder. "I hate her! I don't ever want to see her again as long as I live!"

Cassidy turns to me. "You try."

"Emma," I begin, then stop. What can I tell her? I know exactly how she feels about Zach because I feel the same way. I sigh. "Emma, you're just being silly and you know it. Jess has been your best friend since kindergarten. She's not trying to steal Zach away from you."

Cassidy nods. "That's right. Zach feels comfortable around Jess, that's all. Because they were in the play together. You wouldn't feel this way if he danced with me, would you?"

Emma shakes her head, sniffling. "I guess not."

"That's right. Because you know we're just friends—teammates. Can't you think of Jess and Zach as teammates?"

"I don't know. Maybe."

The door opens and Jess comes flying through it. "What's wrong? Where did you guys all go? Is Emma okay?"

Without thinking I blurt out, "She's having a Zach attack."

This shocks Emma so much she stops crying. She stares at me, horrified. So do Cassidy and Jess. There's a long, uncomfortable silence, and then Emma lets out a little giggle. "I am, aren't I?" she says.

I nod. "Big-time."

A great big belly laugh busts out of Cassidy, and that sets us all off. In the midst of the hilarity, the bathroom door swings open and the Fab Three come in.

"What's so funny?" Becca demands.

"You are," I reply loftily, and we flounce out.

Back in the gym, the four of us huddle together at the edge of the dance floor. Jess looks over at Emma.

"Emma, please understand," she says. "What was I supposed to say when he asked me to dance? I didn't want to hurt his feelings. I know how you feel about Zach, and you've got to believe me that I would never, ever—" She pauses, searching for words. "Look, I've never told you this because it's kind of embarrassing, but I don't even like Zach! Not the way you do. I mean, he's my friend and everything, but I like Darcy!"

Emma gapes at her. "My *brother*?"

Jess nods. "I thought for sure you knew. He's so nice all the time, not just to me, but to everybody. And what he did that night at the play for Sundance, well . . ." She lets the sentence trail off.

Heather Vogel Frederick

"Maybe we should just have fun, and not worry about boys right now," says Cassidy.

"Maybe you're right," I agree.

The music starts up again and Zach drifts over, along with Ethan and Third.

"Wanna dance, Sloane?" Zach asks.

Cassidy winks at Emma. "Sure, why not?"

Ethan asks Jess, leaving Third alone with Emma and me. He looks from one of us to the other in growing panic.

Then Darcy Hawthorne appears. "Mom told me what you did for Emma," he says to me. "Fixing her dress, I mean. That was really nice of you. Would you like to dance?"

I feel very shy all of a sudden. "You don't have to dance with me because of that," I tell him.

He grins. "I'm not," he says. "That outfit of yours is too pretty for you to stand over here by the wall all night. Besides, I'm trying to keep away from Becca Chadwick."

As we move out onto the dance floor, I see Third say something to Emma. She smiles in relief and the two of them head for the refreshment table.

Nobody quite got what they wanted, I think, as I look around at all my friends. But the end result's not bad. Not bad at all.

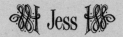 Jess

*"There doesn't seem to be anything to hold on
to when Mother's gone; so I'm all at sea."*

The afternoon starts off like it always does.

I get off the bus, wave to Emma, and pat Sugar, who is, as always, ecstatic to see me. She races me to the house, barking happily and running in excited circles after her tail. The two of us go inside. I grab an apple, then head to my room, where I flip on the TV.

"Hi, Mom!" I say to the screen. Sugar hops up onto the bed beside me and cocks her head as we both examine my mother's outfit. Today she's wearing a red satin dress with sequins, and her dark hair is twisted up into a fancy braid. Soap operas are big on fancy hairdos and sequins. I wonder if my mother likes stuff like that. Most of the time around the farm she just wore her hair tucked up under a baseball cap, and I don't ever remember her wearing sequins.

I take a bite of my apple. "School was fine, Mom, thanks for asking," I say to the screen. Sugar wags her tail. "What? The science test? I aced it."

I take another bite of apple and glance out my bedroom window. I can see the blue glow of the TV screen in my dad's workroom in the barn. He's watching the show too.

Dad doesn't know that I know he watches *HeartBeats*. A few months ago I noticed that he wasn't coming in from the barn to greet me the way he used to when I got home from school. I went out to see what he was doing, and at first I got all excited because I heard mom's voice and I thought she'd finally come home. But when I opened the door to his workroom, it was only the TV.

Dad didn't see me that day, and I've never said a word to him about it. I guess watching the show is just his way of spending a little time with her, same as me. I miss her. A lot. Dylan and Ryan and I went to New York and spent spring break with her, and it was fun and everything—we got to see the Statue of Liberty and the Empire State Building and the Rockettes and all that New York City stuff—but it's just not the same as having her here every day. I don't want to be just a tourist in her new life. I still keep hoping she'll come home.

I turn the volume up a little to hear her voice again, and Mom and Sugar keep me company while I whip through my algebra homework, draw a map of Cortés's voyages for social studies, and read ahead in science to see what we'll be doing next week (oh, boy, frog dissections!). A puff of breeze blows in my window and tickles the back of my neck. I close my science book and look at Sugar. "It's way too nice to be stuck inside, isn't it, girl?"

Sugar's ears prick up. She's hoping I'll take her for a walk or play catch with her in the back yard, but I have something else in mind. I glance over at the TV screen. *HeartBeats* is almost over.

"Bye, Mom!" I say to her. "See you tomorrow." I blow her a kiss and turn off the TV, not bothering to wait for the credits this time. Then I grab Sugar and a quilt and climb out my window onto the back porch roof. This is my secret hiding place. My little brothers haven't discovered it yet, thank goodness. If I lie really still when they're running around the yard, they can't see me, because the roof is nearly flat and they're so short.

I spread the quilt out and Sugar and I lie down on it. It's not summer-warm yet, just spring-warm, but the black shingles on the roof underneath us have been absorbing heat from the sun all afternoon and the quilt quickly grows toasty. I lie back and close my eyes and take a deep breath. Spring is my favorite time of year, and May is my favorite month. Dad's been plowing the fields with Led and Zep, and the smell of the freshly-turned earth is sweeter to me than any flower. I can hear the horses nickering to each other in the paddock. They're huge, but gentle as lambs. Especially Zep. His stall is my other favorite hiding place. This reminds me that I need to muck out both stalls today, plus the goats will need milking soon. I have a lot more chores around here with Mom gone.

But for now I laze just a little bit longer in the sun, breathing in spring. I catch a whiff of lilacs. There's a huge bank of them growing alongside the porch below me. *Syringa vulgaris.* Not a very pretty name for such a pretty flower. Lilacs are my favorite flower. Mom's, too.

I open my eyes and look up at the clouds. *Cumulus, nimbus, cirrus,*

Heather Vogel Frederick

stratus. The names float through my mind in a stately procession. Mom taught them to me. She used to come out here and join me sometimes, when she wasn't too busy. We'd watch the clouds, and she'd tell me their proper scientific terms, and then we'd decide what they looked like. Dragons and sailing ships, mermaids and movie stars and flocks of sheep. Mom never told anyone about my secret hiding place, not even Dad. I made her promise she wouldn't, and she kept that promise.

I wonder if she'll keep her promise to Dad. "Just a few months, Michael," I heard her tell him, the night before she left. "Just give me a few months to figure this all out."

It's been nearly a year.

I decide that the cloud over the barn looks like a teapot. Definitely a cumulus. *Cumulus congestus,* in fact, because it's so massive and puffy. I love science, and the way it names and orders and classifies everything, from clouds to plants to stars. Even bones. *Tibia, fibula, scapula, patella.* Science makes everything so official-sounding, and so tidy. Unlike real life, which is often a mess.

Next to science I like math, for the same reason. Music, too. Mom was the one who pointed out to me how much math and music have in common. The orderly arrangement of notes, that sort of thing. But the sense of order is not the only reason I like music. I like it because—well, because it's like it's a part of me, a part of who I am. I feel alive when I sing.

Reading is okay, but it's not my favorite. I'd rather actually do something than just read about it. But I have to admit I like *Little Women*. I didn't think I would, but I do. I like feisty, independent Jo and her sisters, and especially Marmee. Marmee is so dependable. Marmee would never leave her family, no matter how confused she was about life.

Which reminds me. Book club is meeting here tonight at Half Moon Farm for the very first time. How could I have forgotten? I scramble up and climb back into my bedroom, lifting Sugar through the window after me. I glance at the clock on my bedside table. Nearly an hour before the twins get home from T-ball practice. There's still enough time to straighten up the house and bake some cookies before I have to start my chores. I want to be sure and leave time for a shower, too. Even though Megan's no longer one of the Fab Four, I still don't want to give her any reason to think of me as Goat Girl. Or Princess Jess of Ramshackle Farm.

Downstairs, I'm surprised to find that the house is already tidy. There aren't any chicken droppings on the kitchen floor, and everything's been dusted and vacuumed and neatened. Not only that, but there's a platter of cookies—snickerdoodles, my all-time favorite—on top of the fridge out of my little brothers' reach, and inside there's a jug of homemade lemonade. Taped to it is a little note: "DO NOT TOUCH! FOR BOOK CLUB!" I smile. Nice try, but a note's not going to stop the twins. A bouquet of lilacs is on the kitchen table, and now that I look closely, I can tell that even Sugar has had a good brushing. Dad's been busy today.

The back door swings shut with a loud snap.

Heather Vogel Frederick

"Hi, honey," my father says. His eyes are red and he looks like maybe he's been crying.

"Hey, Dad," I reply, pretending not to notice. "Thanks for picking up the house. It looks nice."

He smiles. "Special night tonight."

I raise my eyebrows at him. Book club's not that special. But I nod and head out to the barn to start my chores.

After my shower and dinner, everyone arrives all at once.

"What a wonderful old house!" says Mrs. Sloane, looking around curiously. This is the first time she's been here.

"Thank you," my father replies. "It's been in my family since the Revolutionary War."

"That's what Jess told me. Amazing."

As I start to herd everyone into the living room, my dad holds up his hand. "Ladies," he announces. "In view of the fact that it is such a delightful spring evening, may I invite you to accompany me to the lilac arbor?"

Megan Wong shoots me a glance that clearly says "You Delaneys are so weird," and I feel myself turning red. What arbor is my dad talking about? We don't have an arbor! I reluctantly follow him outside and everybody else follows me as he leads us around to the far side of the house.

"Welcome," he says proudly.

Standing there is a contraption made of white plastic pipes from the sprinkler system he's been working on. My dad has curved long pieces over like arches, then lashed the ends down to old tent pegs.

Onto each arch he's woven branches of lilacs. It's pretty, actually, but definitely odd. I can only imagine what Megan is thinking. It looks like something you'd see at an outdoor wedding. A very funky, hippie wedding.

"Michael, it's lovely!" says Mrs. Sloane. "So quaint. Whatever gave you the idea?"

My father shrugs modestly, but he looks pleased. "I thought it fit with the whole Louisa May Alcott theme, you know? Didn't she write a book called *Under the Lilacs*?"

Mrs. Hawthorne nods approvingly. "She certainly did."

There are eight lawn chairs set up in a circle beneath the arches of flowers. We take our seats and Mrs. Hawthorne gives us the handouts.

Cassidy laughs aloud at this month's "In Her Own Words" quote: "I'd rather be a free spinster and paddle my own canoe."

"Louisa May Alcott is my kind of woman," she says.

"Hush," says her mother. "Just you wait. Someday you may change your mind. Life's more fun on a bicycle built for two than traveling solo in a canoe."

Fun Facts About Louisa

1. Louisa May Alcott never married.
2. She modeled Meg's wedding in *Little Women* after that of her sister Anna.
3. In later life, after her sister May's death, Louisa became a foster parent to May's little daughter Lulu.

Heather Vogel Frederick

We talk for a while about this month's assigned reading, when Amy and Laurie surprise everyone by getting married in Europe after Beth dies. Pretty much everybody has something to say, even Cassidy, who is usually grumpy. She tells us about the time she went to Europe, too, just like Amy. Only it was for a hockey tournament, not to study art.

"And I didn't fall in love, either," she says belligerently.

Megan's been too, of course. Only Emma and I haven't been. Except for my trips to New York this year to visit Mom, I've barely been out of Massachusetts.

"Would you ladies care for some refreshments?" asks my father, when there's a pause in the conversation. I'm not sure what's gotten into him. He's talking like someone out of a book. So formal.

"That would be lovely," says Emma's mom, sounding equally formal.

"Jess, would you do the honors?" he asks me. "There's something I need to get from the barn."

Wondering what surprise he's going to produce next—hopefully not a goat, as Megan and I are still on slightly shaky ground where goats are concerned—I fetch the tray of lemonade and cookies.

As I'm passing it around, my dad returns with a long pole draped with ribbons and a huge paper bag. He hands the paper bag to me.

"Is it your birthday, Jess?" asks Mrs. Sloane curiously.

I shake my head no. I look over at my dad. He just folds his arms across his chest and smiles. Something very strange is going on.

"Well, go ahead," says Cassidy. "Open the bag."

Inside are four lilac wreaths and a tambourine. I pull them out and we all stare at them, puzzled. Before anyone can say anything, my dad takes one of the wreaths and holds it above my head.

Megan's wearing her you-Delaneys-are-nuts expression again, and Cassidy and Emma are both watching us, wide-eyed. My father places the wreath on my head, then reaches for the tambourine and gives it a shake. He motions to Emma, Cassidy, and Megan and they stand up reluctantly and move over next to me. My father puts a lilac wreath on each of their heads too. Then he pulls a notecard out of the back pocket of his jeans and clears his throat.

"Today we celebrate springtide," he announces, jangling the tambourine again. "The springtide not only of the year, but the springtide of life for these four maidens as well."

Cassidy, Emma, Megan, and I look at one another in horrified silence. Under the arbor, Mrs. Hawthorne's lips are pressed tightly together. Megan's mother is suddenly very busy patting Sugar. Mrs. Sloane has covered her mouth with her hand. They're trying not to laugh.

My dad doesn't notice. He's too busy fitting the beribboned pole into a hole in the ground that he's obviously dug for that specific purpose. He turns around, beaming triumphantly, hands us each one of the long ribbons dangling from it, and gives the tambourine a prolonged rattle. "Let the celebration begin!" he cries.

None of us move an inch. Under my lilac wreath, my face is beet red.

"What celebration?" asks Mrs. Hawthorne, finally.

Heather Vogel Frederick

The tambourine falters. "The, uh—you know—" My father looks over at Mrs. Wong and Mrs. Sloane, who are shaking with silent laughter. "What's so funny?" he asks in an injured tone.

He pulls something else out of his back pocket. It's a magazine. I cringe when I see the title. *Motherhood Monthly.* He started subscribing to it after Mom left. It's some dumb hippie thing with all sorts of lame advice on raising kids. And really terrible recipes that only Mrs. Wong would like. My dad points to the cover. "I read about it in this month's issue," he explains. "See? It says right here: 'The Dance of the Maypole Maidens.' I thought it sounded—" He looks at us all reproachfully. "I thought it sounded like fun." His voice trails off.

My eyes well up with tears. Our first chance to host the book club, and my father has to ruin it with some stupid ritual. Everyone's right—my family is weird!

There's a rustling in the bushes behind us. We all turn around to see Ryan emerge. He's been spying on us. He grins. There's a gap where his two front teeth usually reside. "Aren't you going to dance, Jess?"

Mrs. Hawthorne and Mrs. Wong and Mrs. Sloane explode with laughter. So do Megan and Emma and Cassidy.

I let out a sob and rip the lilac crown off my head. Shut up!" I scream. "Shut up, shut up, shut up, shut UP!"

I race toward the house. I've never felt so totally humiliated in my entire life, not even after the fiasco with Sundance.

Behind me I hear my dad calling. "Jess!" he says. "Come on, sweetheart. I didn't mean to—I just I thought—"

The back door slams shut behind me and I never find out what he thought. I don't care. I hate him and I hate this stupid book club and I hate lilacs and most of all I hate Mom for not being here. I pound up the stairs to my room and throw myself on the bed, sobbing.

I'm still sobbing a few minutes later when I hear the door creak open. "Go away!" I cry.

"It's just us," says Emma. "Well, and Sugar."

Sugar leaps up onto the bed beside me and starts to lick my face. I know there's a scientific explanation for this, that it's only the salt from my tears that she wants, but right now I prefer to think that she's licking me because she loves me. Sugar is the best dog in the whole world. She'd never humiliate me in front of my friends. I put my arm around her and bury my face in her soft fur.

Emma and Megan and Cassidy are still standing in the doorway.

"Go away," I repeat.

"Jess, your father didn't mean to hurt your feelings," says Emma. "He's just, well, you know. Trying to be a good parent. While your mother's away, I mean."

I lift my head and glare at her. I don't need Emma or anyone else reminding me that my mother's not here.

"C'mon, Jess, it's not that bad," says Cassidy.

"How would you know?"

"You think you've got it bad, just imagine what it's like being related to a supermodel!" she replies. "Everywhere we go, people point and

Heather Vogel Frederick

whisper. Or ask for her autograph. Or stare at me like I'm some kind of freak because I don't look a bit like her."

"And don't you think my mother embarrasses me sometimes?" Megan's dark almond eyes are serious. She sits down on the edge of my bed. "How about all her stupid causes? And remember the carrot crunchies at last month's book club meeting?"

"Those horrible cookies?" Cassidy shudders at the memory. "Cheer up, Jess. At least your dad serves decent snacks."

"My mother says it's every parent's job to embarrass their children," adds Emma.

"Great," I mutter. "My dad sure succeeded." I roll over onto my back and stare up at the ceiling. "I just can't believe he did that."

"You have to admit, it was kind of funny," says Emma. "Those weird lilac wreaths and everything, I mean."

"A crown for Princess Jess of Ramshackle Farm," I reply bitterly. "I'm just glad Becca Chadwick wasn't here to see me. I'd never hear the end of it."

Cassidy strikes a pose and pretends to jangle a tambourine. "The Dance of the Maypole Maidens," she intones.

Megan lets out a little snicker, and pretty soon the bed is shaking because I'm giggling too.

I sit up and blow my nose. Sugar barks. I'm starting to feel a little better.

"So were we really supposed to hold hands and dance around the maypole and everything?" Emma asks.

Cassidy leaps up into the air in a clumsy pirouette.

"What's a maypole?" asks Dylan, crawling out from underneath my bed.

"You little CREEP!" I holler, grabbing him by his hair and hauling him to his feet. "Get out! And quit spying on me!" I throw him out into the hallway and slam the door shut and lock it. "Little brothers are the *worst*!"

I turn around. My friends are laughing. At first I don't think it's funny, then all of a sudden I'm laughing too. The four of us join hands in a circle ands whirl around the room. Sugar barks ecstatically, leaping and wriggling as she tries to join in our wild dance.

We collapse on the bed in a breathless pile, still laughing. There's a knock on the door. My dad pokes his head into the room.

"Um, could I talk to you, Jess?" he asks.

My friends file swiftly out of the room. Emma gives me a thumbs-up, then closes the door behind her.

I busy myself stroking Sugar's soft fur. My dad hesitantly takes a seat at the end of the bed.

"Jess, sweetheart, I'm so sorry. I didn't mean—"

"I know, Dad. It's okay."

"No, it's not," he says. "It's just that, with your mother away and all, I'm having to do things I never had to before. Not just run the farm by myself, but try to take care of you and your brothers properly too." We're both quiet for a moment. I know that what he's telling me is true. "I'm just so sorry that I embarrassed you," he continues finally. "I

Heather Vogel Frederick

should have known better, but that blasted magazine made it sound so matter-of-fact. Like something all girls your age do. The Dance of the Maypole Maidens, I mean."

A smile creeps across my lips. My father looks at me hopefully. "But I guess it's not, huh?"

I shake my head. A giggle escapes. "Dad, what were you thinking? A *tambourine*?"

He whips the magazine out of his back pocket. "It says so right here!" he cries, eyes widening in mock indignation. "See? Items needed: floral crowns, one maypole, one tambourine."

We both burst out laughing, and I throw my arms around him.

"I love you so much, Jess," my father whispers, hugging me tightly. "I wish your mother were here to help you through all these growing pains, but she's not, and I'm doing the best I can."

"I know you are, Dad," I whisper back. "I love you, too."

He hands me a tissue and I blow my nose, and then we go back downstairs to where our friends are waiting for us under the lilacs.

SUMMER

"*Mothers may differ in their management, but the hope is the same in all—the desire to see their children happy.*"

—Little Women

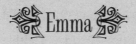

Emma

"You can't say nothing pleasant ever happens now, can you?"

I love the last day of school.

This year I'm doubly happy—first, that sixth grade is almost officially over and that means I don't have to start worrying about seventh grade for nearly three whole months, and second, that today is my birthday. I'm finally twelve, just like Jess and Megan and Cassidy. I think I was the last person in the whole sixth grade to turn twelve.

The bus is late. Darcy picks up a stick and practices his baseball swing. I take out my Mother-Daughter Book Club journal and work on my latest poem, which is not about Zach Norton.

Finally, the bus lumbers into view. I climb aboard behind my brother. Becca Chadwick looks me up and down, as usual.

"Nice sundress, Emma!" she calls, her voice oozing sarcasm. Ashley starts to snicker. I could practically set my watch by those two lame-brains.

I find myself wishing Cassidy were here. "Buzz, buzz, buzz," she'd say, and laugh it off. It's not easy for me, though. I slide into a seat and automatically start to hunch down. Then my gaze falls on the bookmark in my notebook. *"I am not afraid of storms, for I am learning how to sail my ship."* Louisa May Alcott would not let a moron like Becca Chadwick spoil her birthday. Neither would Jo March. I straighten up, turn around, and look Becca right in the eye. "Thanks for noticing," I call back. "Nicole Patterson gave it to me. Wasn't that nice of her?"

For once, Becca doesn't know what to say. So for once, she doesn't say anything at all. I turn around again and look out the window and smile. My birthday is off to a good start.

The bus trundles past meadows fresh with the promise of summer and eventually comes to a stop in front of Half Moon Farm. Jess slides in beside me. "Happy Birthday, Em!" she says, giving me a hug. "I can hardly wait for the party." The Mother-Daughter Book Club is throwing me a party this afternoon at the Wongs'. I'm hoping Mrs. Wong isn't in charge of the cake.

We spend the rest of the bus ride talking about what we're going to do over the summer. Mostly we just plan to hang out at Half Moon Farm like we always do. It's the best. We ride Led and Zep and gather eggs and help make goat cheese and raspberry jam and stuff for the farm stand, and when we get tired of chores there's the creek beyond the edge of the fields to splash around in and Walden Pond to swim in. Jess knows every trail through the woods, and the names of every bird, insect, and flower. Last summer, she taught me how to gather milkweed before it dries into pods, and to boil the

Heather Vogel Frederick

flower buds in water on the stove. They're delicious with butter and salt. Once, we found an arrowhead, and I keep hoping I'll find something from the Revolutionary War—the button from a minuteman's uniform, maybe, or an old coin. That would be so amazing.

This year, we're thinking about making a secret hideout in the barn, someplace the twins can't find us. There's a tack room up by the hayloft that doesn't get used much, and Mr. Delaney said Jess and I could have it. It sounds like the perfect retreat for a poet, and we figure we'd invite Megan and Cassidy over for a campout once we get it all fixed up.

The last day of classes goes by quickly—mostly it's just parties and teachers passing back all the assignments they've collected from us over the year, and turning in our library fines and stuff like that. We have a sixth grade kickball tournament out on the baseball diamond, and our homeroom beats the pants off Mr. Flanagan's, thanks to Cassidy and Zach. My birthday luck seems to be holding because I don't do too horribly, for once, and Zach even gives me a high five after I manage to kick the ball way out into left field when the bases are loaded, bringing home two runs. A high five may not be as good as a dance in the gym, but still, it's something.

Then it's time to go. Jess and Cassidy and I ride Megan's bus home with her, because of my party.

"Come in, come in!" says Mrs. Wong, greeting us at the door.

Mom and Mrs. Sloane are already there, drinking iced tea, and so is Mr. Delaney. He's traded his usual jeans for slacks, and he's wearing a crisply ironed blue shirt. His hair is wet, like he just took a shower, and when he hugs me I notice that there's not even a whiff of barnyard on him. He smells good, like aftershave.

"Happy birthday, Emma," he says.

"Thanks, Mr. Delaney."

I glance past him into the dining room, which is decorated with crepe paper streamers and balloons. A big banner with "HAPPY 12th BIRTHDAY, EMMA!" on it is hanging across the window, and I spot a pile of presents waiting for me in the middle of the table.

"Uh-uh-uh," says Mrs. Wong. "No peeking. You girls go put your things in Megan's room while Mrs. Sloane finishes decorating the cake."

I'm delighted to obey, especially now that I know Mrs. Sloane is making the cake. I was worried I might have to be all polite about some horrible sugar-free tofu creation, but Mrs. Sloane is an even better cook than my dad. She could have her own TV show, I swear.

We troop down the long hallway to Megan's room, where we dump our backpacks, then she gives us a tour of the new sewing room that her mother set up for her "hobby," as she calls it, in the old guest bedroom next door. Mrs. Wong will probably never give up hope that Megan will grow up to be an environmental engineer or rainforest activist or something, but still, the sewing room is a step in the right direction.

"Wow," I say when we return to the dining room, and I mean it. The table looks beautiful. There's a white linen tablecloth on it, and a big white jug filled with fragrant pink roses from Mrs. Sloane's garden. Fresh strawberries from Half Moon Farm are heaped in a bowl beside plates of tiny sandwiches ("Made with organic cucumbers," says Mrs.

Heather Vogel Frederick

Wong proudly) and there's a platter of my dad's special oatmeal cookies, too. The centerpiece is Mrs. Sloane's cake, which is frosted with pink frosting and decorated with little white flowers—real ones!—and geranium leaves that she makes us all smell because they're lemon-scented. Plus, there's both strawberry and vanilla ice cream from Kimball Farm, and pink lemonade to drink.

"Too much pink," grumbles Cassidy.

"It's perfect," I sigh.

Everybody sings "Happy Birthday" to me, and I blow out the candles and then we sit down and start to eat. Even though this afternoon is not an official Mother-Daughter Book Club meeting—it's over for the year, now that we've finished the book—we end up talking about *Little Women* anyway. Mostly, we argue about whether Jo should have married Laurie instead of Professor Bhaer. My mother and I both think Jo and Laurie should have ended up together.

"Louisa copped out on her readers," my mother says heatedly. "She knew that's what we all wanted, but for whatever reason, she didn't want to give us that happy ending. So she married Laurie off to Amy instead, and threw in Professor Bhaer at the last minute."

"I disagree," says Mr. Delaney, taking a bite of cake. "I like Bhaer. Plus, wasn't he modeled after Louisa's father?"

We take a vote, and it's a split decision. Four for Jo and Laurie, four for Jo and Professor Bhaer.

"Just like real life," says Mr. Delaney lightly. "You can't always predict the end of the story."

Finally, it's time for presents. There's a whole stack of poetry books from my parents, and from Cassidy and her mother an awesome fountain pen that uses real ink ("It was my mother's idea, not mine," says Cassidy ungraciously). Jess and her father give me a rhyming dictionary, and from Megan and her mother there's a beautiful purple velvet mood pillow.

"Megan made it," says Mrs. Wong. "We figured if Louisa had one, an aspiring writer like you should have one too."

I stand it on its end to show that I am in a good mood, which I certainly am after all these presents, and everyone laughs.

"There's one more gift for you," says Mr. Delaney, rising to his feet.

"I hope it's not a tambourine," says Cassidy in a stage whisper.

Jess's father grins. "Definitely not a tambourine," he replies. "This one is actually from Shannon, and it's for all of you girls." He passes us each an envelope.

"Shannon wanted to do something special for the four of you," my mother says. "She asked us what we thought, and we got to talking after yoga class a few weeks ago—"

"Uh-oh," I reply automatically.

"Emma!" my mother says, exasperated. "For heaven's sake! You haven't even opened it yet."

I turn to Jess. "Do you know what it is?"

She shakes her head. "No clue."

"Can we open them?" asks Cassidy.

"All together on the count of three," says her mother. "One, two . . ."

I tear open my envelope on "three" and pull out a train ticket. Four of them, actually. I stare at them blankly. "Boston to New York, round trip, first class," I read. I look up at my mother, who is smiling broadly. Mrs. Sloane takes a picture of my astonished expression. "Wow!" I say. "Are we really going to New York?"

Our mothers all nod happily.

"Check it out!" calls Cassidy, waving something in the air. "She got us tickets to a Yankees game!"

"And to *Little Women: The Musical*," Megan says. "A Broadway show! Jess, your mom rocks!"

"What's in your envelope, honey?" my mother asks Jess.

She holds up a brochure, a wary look on her face. "We're staying at a hotel," she replies. "Someplace called the Pierre." She looks over at her father. "How come we're not staying with Mom?"

"That's because . . . you three ladies are going too!" he cries, tossing envelopes at my mother and Mrs. Sloane and Mrs. Wong.

"Oh, my," says my mother, a bit breathlessly. "I really can't—it's much too expensive—Michael, she shouldn't have!"

Mr. Delaney smiles. "It's a done deal, Phoebe. There's no dissuading Shannon when she gets a bee in her bonnet about something." He winks at Mrs. Wong. "Besides, from what I hear, the enterprise received a generous charitable contribution from a local benefactor."

Now it's Mrs. Wong's turn to smile. "It's a worthy cause," she says.

My mother and Mrs. Sloane jump up and hug her.

"Are you going too, Dad?" asks Jess.

Mr. Delaney shakes his head. "Nope. I'll be holding down the fort here at home with the twins."

"But—"

He waves away her concern. "It's a girls' trip, sweetie. Your mother has all sorts of stuff planned—you know, manicures, shopping, that sort of thing. Not my scene."

Jess still doesn't look convinced. Across the room, my mother and Mrs. Wong and Mrs. Sloane have formed a conga line. They reach out and grab Cassidy and Megan and Jess and me and we all dance down the hall into the Wongs' enormous living room.

"It's not a maypole, but it will do," says Mr. Delaney, chasing after us with the camera. "Look out, New York—the Mother-Daughter Book Club is coming to town!"

Heather Vogel Frederick

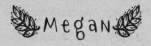

Megan

"Women work a great many miracles."

"Oh, great, look who's here," groans Emma. "Wouldn't you know it."

We're standing on the depot platform, waiting to catch the commuter train to Boston where we'll transfer to Amtrak for New York City. I don't need to turn around to see whom Emma's spotted. I can tell just by the look on her face. But I do anyway, and sure enough, there's Becca Chadwick heading our way. Her mother is right behind her.

"Well, if it isn't Concord's most exclusive club," booms Mrs. Chadwick. She looks us over sourly, her eyes narrowing as she spies our luggage. "Going on a trip, are you?"

Mrs. Hawthorne nods. "That's right, Calliope," she replies evenly. "New York City."

"Dreadful place," says Becca's mother dismissively. "So crowded. And wretchedly hot this time of year." She casts a calculating glance at Jess. "Any word yet on when your mother's going to quit that ridiculous television show and come home to Half Moon Farm?"

There's an awkward silence. Jess stares down at her sandals. Mrs. Hawthorne places a protective hand on her shoulder.

"Shannon will be meeting our train in New York," she says icily. "Perhaps you'd like us to relay your question directly to her?"

Mrs. Chadwick bridles at this, but before she can retort there's the sharp screech of metal on metal as the commuter train pulls into the station.

"Let's go, girls!" says Mrs. Sloane, grabbing her suitcase.

We all follow her on board. Mrs. Chadwick wedges herself into the empty seat beside Emma's mother, who is wearing a slightly faded summer dress that I'm guessing she got at the thrift store. Across from her, Mrs. Sloane is dressed exquisitely in a white dress with a black patent-leather belt, black strappy sandals, and a broad-brimmed black straw hat. Only my mother isn't wearing a dress. She opted for shorts and a T-shirt (this one's slogan reads "Certified Tree Hugger") instead.

"So where are you two off to this morning?" Mrs. Sloane asks Becca's mother, her voice all sugary-polite.

"The orthodontist," Mrs. Chadwick informs her. "Rebecca has an overbite."

Our heads all swivel as we turn to inspect Rebecca, who glares at us.

Cassidy grins, revealing perfectly straight teeth. "Tough luck."

"Metal-mouth," I whisper softly, so Mrs. Chadwick can't hear.

My mother hears, though. She gives me the evil-witch-mother eye of death, and I sigh and turn around and face front again.

Heather Vogel Frederick

"Any vacation plans this summer?" asks my mother.

"Cleveland," barks Mrs. Chadwick.

"Ah," says Mrs. Hawthorne. "That's a very, uh, educational place, from what I hear."

Mrs. Chadwick nods smugly. "Much more appropriate for young girls than"—she pauses and gives a delicate shudder, or as delicate a shudder as someone the size of an orca can manage—"New York."

"Lots of museums in Cleveland," says Mrs. Hawthorne.

"And of course the symphony," adds my mother.

"Indeed," agrees Mrs. Chadwick. "Becca and Stewart will be exposed to a wide range of cultural activities in Cleveland."

Cassidy and Jess and Emma and I all turn around and grin at Becca, who looks like she just swallowed a jar of pickle juice.

"Mmm," says Mrs. Hawthorne, winking at Emma. "Cultural activities are always very edifying."

Emma perks up. "That's right, Mrs. Chadwick," she chirps. "So instructive."

"Broadening," adds my mother.

"Uplifting," offers Mrs. Sloane, smiling broadly.

"Dull," whispers Cassidy wickedly, slanting a glance over the seat at Becca, who shoots her a murderous look in return.

"Yawn," breathes Jess.

"Snoozer," I add softly, rubbing it in.

"Nothing frivolous about Cleveland, no sirree," says Mrs. Sloane cheerfully, whipping out our itinerary. "Nothing as uneducational as—let's see, what is it we're doing again? Oh, yes. Visiting the fashion director at *Flash,* one of the magazines where I used to model; going to a ballgame at Yankee Stadium; having lunch on the set of *HeartBeats*; and getting makeovers by their stylist before we head to Broadway for a show."

"Don't forget shopping," says Mrs. Hawthorne.

"Or staying at a fancy hotel," says my mother.

Mrs. Chadwick gives a haughty sniff and heaves herself out of her seat. "Come along, Becca," she orders. "I'm sure we can find seats near a better class of passengers."

"Now, that's what I'd call a caboose," says Mrs. Hawthorne quietly, eyeing Mrs. Chadwick's retreating hindquarters.

"Why, Phoebe Hawthorne!" cries Mrs. Sloane in delight. "I didn't know you had it in you!"

Mrs. Hawthorne blushes, then giggles. "Neither did I," she replies. She gives Emma a guilty glance. "Don't tell your father."

We're all still laughing when our train pulls into the station. Outside on the platform, we pass the Chadwicks.

"Have fun in Cleveland!" I call to Becca.

"And at the orthodontist!" adds Cassidy, baring her teeth again as Mrs. Chadwick waddles away, towing a deflated-looking Becca behind her.

Our spirits high—the trip to New York is off to a good start—we find our train and the first-class car. Our mothers quickly settle into conversation. Emma gets out a book, Cassidy practices her hook shot by tossing balls of crumpled-up paper into a trash can, and Jess looks

Heather Vogel Frederick

out the window and hums happily to herself. I pull out my sketchbook and start designing new outfits for my friends.

For Emma, who is wearing shorts that are too tight and a flower-splashed blouse that is just as ugly as it was when she wore it last summer, I dream up a graceful sundress whose flowing lines conceal her round tummy. I leave her halo of brown curls just the way it is, as the style suits her. The first thing I do for Jess, on the other hand, is release her hair from its usual thick braid and let it settle around her shoulders. Then I draw her in a short, sassy skirt with a scoop-necked polka-dot blouse. I eye it critically, then add a ruffle to the neckline. Perfect.

It has to be pants for Cassidy, of course, so I create a pair of chic overall shorts and pair them with a sailor-style shirt boyish enough that Cassidy might actually wear it, yet still feminine. As for her hair, I choose a sleek bob cut just below her jawline, a huge improvement over the tangled mass she usually just scrapes back into a ponytail.

I'm so absorbed in my task that the trip passes quickly, and before we know it we're in New York and Mrs. Delaney is running alongside the train, tapping on the window and waving wildly to Jess.

Mrs. Delaney is really pretty. She looks a lot like Jess—same blue eyes, same slender build—but her hair is dark instead of blonde. She's dressed a lot differently than I remember, too. Last time I saw her, she was wearing jeans and a T-shirt and a baseball cap. Now, she's dressed in crisply tailored pink linen capris and an ultrafeminine sheer white blouse. Like Mrs. Sloane, she's wearing strappy sandals, only hers are white instead of black. I make a mental note to add her to my sketchbook at the hotel.

A quick cab ride uptown gets us to our destination, where a bell-hop takes our luggage and whisks us upstairs to our room.

Rooms, actually. Mrs. Delaney has booked two of them, one for the moms and one for us, with a connecting door between them.

"Wow," whispers Emma as she looks around, awed.

"I made sure you had a view of Central Park," says Mrs. Delaney proudly, pulling back the curtains.

"It's perfect, Shannon, just perfect," says Mrs. Hawthorne, sinking into an armchair with a contented sigh and gazing dreamily at the green oasis spread out below us.

Cassidy leaps gleefully onto one of the luxurious beds and starts jumping up and down. "I could stay here forever!" she crows.

"Cassidy Ann, behave yourself," snaps her mother.

Next stop is Mrs. Delaney's apartment for lunch. It's just a few blocks away in a neighborhood she calls the Upper West Side. It's tiny, but it has a view of the Hudson River. Spice, the Delaneys' other sheltie, goes nuts when she sees Jess.

"You miss your sister, don't you?" murmurs Jess. She gives Spice a kiss. "That's from Sugar. She misses you, too."

After lunch, it's time for shopping. As we walk over to Fifth Avenue, my head is practically swiveling. Everywhere I turn I see something I want to sketch. I can't shop and draw at the same time, though, so I leave my sketchbook in my purse and gawk instead. New York is teeming with sleek, elegant women—some of them just have to be

Heather Vogel Frederick

models—and the store windows are amazing, all of them crammed with incredibly fashionable clothes that must cost a fortune.

Mrs. Sloane and Mrs. Delaney know all the good places to shop, and they run our legs off for three solid hours. Finally, loaded with bags and parcels, we stuff ourselves into a pair of taxis and head downtown.

"Wolfgang!" cries Mrs. Sloane as a tall, thin man dressed entirely in black emerges from the elevator at *Flash* magazine.

"Clementine, darling, it's been far too long," he replies, crossing the lobby and kissing her on both cheeks. "You look gorgeous, as usual." He turns to Mrs. Delaney. "And Shannon O'Halloran! We met at the Soap Bubble Awards party last winter. Enchanting to see you again."

He turns to the rest of us, his forehead wrinkling in a slightly pained expression as he catches sight of our outfits. Well, everyone's outfit but mine. His eyebrows shoot up as he examines my gypsy skirt, off-the-shoulder T-shirt, and hoop earrings. He purses his lips and gives me a nod. I feel a warm glow inside. The fashion director of *Flash* approves of me! I follow along happily as our tour begins.

Every atom in my body is on full alert as we wander the hallways of the magazine's busy headquarters. We pass racks and racks of clothes, and walls covered with swatches of fabric and design sketches. People are running around importantly clutching clipboards, and now and then a head pops out of a doorway as we go by. Everywhere I hear whispers: *Clementine.* Mrs. Sloane swans along like a queen, nodding at her fawning subjects and graciously posing for photographs.

My mother looks like she's landed on a different planet. Kind of bewildered and disapproving at the same time. Me, on the other hand—well, I've never felt so alive in my entire life. I feel like I've come home. *This is my world,* I think, pinching myself to be sure I'm not dreaming. *This will be me someday.* I'm smiling so hard my face feels like it's going to crack.

We end up in a conference room, where Wolfgang's assistant appears with a tray of sparkling water for us.

"By the way, Megan, did you happen to bring your sketchbook with you?" Mrs. Sloane asks.

Surprised, I nod. She holds out her hand and I fish it out of my bag.

"There's something I'd like you to see, Wolfgang," Mrs. Sloane says.

The room is silent for a few minutes except for the sound of *Flash*'s fashion director turning the pages of my sketchbook. Finally, he closes it and looks up.

"How old are you?" he asks me.

"Um, twelve," I reply. I can feel my face turning scarlet.

"Extraordinary," he says. He stands up abruptly. "Excuse me for a moment."

Wolfgang returns shortly, accompanied by an icicle-thin woman with a shock of hair dyed an outrageous shade of orange. She's draped in beads and bangles and bracelets, and she regards us through enormous electric-blue eyeglasses. I recognize her instantly.

Her eyes light up when she spots Mrs. Sloane. "Clementine!"

Mrs. Sloane springs to her feet. "Isabelle! I thought you were in Paris."

"I just returned yesterday."

Heather Vogel Frederick

The two of them exchange air kisses, and then Mrs. Sloane turns to us. "This is Isabelle d'Azur, editor in chief of *Flash*."

Isabelle inclines her head regally at us. Wolfgang hands her my notebook. Again, the room falls silent. She examines it carefully, and when she's finished, she peers at me thoughtfully through her vibrant glasses. Then she looks at Wolfgang. "Are you thinking what I'm thinking?" she asks him.

Wolfgang nods. "Fresh, young, very hip," he murmurs. "Perfect."

"Tell me your name," Isabelle d'Azur demands.

"Megan Wong," I whisper, wondering if I've done something wrong.

She turns to my mother. Her forehead wrinkles with the same pained expression Wolfgang's did when he first caught sight of her T-shirt. "A tree hugger," she murmurs. "How admirable. Ah, Mrs. Wong, we are in the process of starting a spin-off magazine for teens. We're calling it *Flashlite*, and we're looking for promising young teen designers to profile for our first issue. I think your daughter would be a perfect fit."

The air rushes out of my lungs. Nothing in the world could have prepared me for this. Across the table, Cassidy gives me a thumbs-up. Emma and Jess beam. Mrs. Sloane looks like the cat who ate the canary.

"We'd need your permission, of course," adds Wolfgang.

"Well, I, uh—" My mother is clearly as surprised as me.

I still can't speak, but I reach over and grab her hand and squeeze it with all my might. If she says anything about MIT or Harvard right now, I think I'll burst into tears. She looks at me and sighs. She shakes her head. My heart nearly stops until I see that she's smiling. "Of course," she says. "What a wonderful opportunity for my daughter."

I float back to the hotel, completely unaware of the taxi or the traffic or the excited conversation buzzing around me. Isabelle d'Azur, editor in chief of *Flash* magazine, called me a "promising young designer"!

I'm still floating as we change into casual clothes for the Yankees game. Well, all of us except Emma and Cassidy and my mother, who are already wearing casual clothes.

"There's one for everyone," says Cassidy, rummaging in her suitcase and pulling out a stack of Red Sox caps. "Mom and I got them for us."

"We're probably taking our lives in our hands, wearing these to Yankee Stadium," laughs Mrs. Delaney, pulling hers on.

At the ballpark, we get hot dogs and sodas and find our seats. The game starts, and while everybody else watches, I replay every moment of our visit to *Flash* in my head. All of a sudden, there's a commotion around me and I notice that the crowd is on its feet. I look around, blinking. Beside me, Cassidy is standing on her chair.

"It's mine!" she cries, leaping into the air. She lands on a man standing in front of us, who good-naturedly sets her on her feet and claps her on her back.

"Good job, kid," he says. "Looks like this is your lucky day."

"I got it!" screams Cassidy, nearly beside herself with excitement.

"Got what?" I ask, still bewildered.

"Weren't you watching?" Emma shouts. She points to the giant TV screen across the field, where they're replaying Cassidy's leap. "She caught a foul ball!"

Not just any foul ball, as it turns out. While I was daydreaming, the

Heather Vogel Frederick

Red Sox came up to bat, and apparently anyone who catches a foul ball can get it autographed by the players. So Cassidy now owns a ball signed by her favorite baseball team. Who ended up beating the Yankees, to boot. She talks about it all the way back to the hotel.

Back in our room, she leaps up onto the bed. "I have an announcement to make!" she cries, holding up her prize.

"Cassidy Ann, I thought I warned you about jumping on the bed," her mother says.

"I'm not jumping, I'm standing," Cassidy replies indignantly. "It's different."

Her mother sighs, and perches on the arm of the chair where my mother is sitting. "Okay, then, out with it."

"This was the most perfect day *ever*," says Cassidy. She pulls me up beside her. "Right, Megan?"

I give a little bounce. My mother shoots me the evil-witch-mother eye of death. I stop bouncing. "Absolutely," I agree, grinning.

Mrs. Sloane stands up. She climbs onto the bed with Cassidy and me. "If you can't beat 'em, join 'em, right?" she says. "Actually, I have an announcement to make too."

We all stare at her expectantly.

"Tomorrow morning, before we go to the set of *HeartBeats*, you are all invited to breakfast at the Food Network," she says. "It's a little celebration for a new TV show. A show called"—she pauses dramatically—"*Cooking with Clementine!*"

Everyone stares at her, speechless.

"You mean, cooking with *you*?" blurts Cassidy.

Her mother nods happily. "And decorating and gardening, too. It's been in the works for a while now," she tells us. "Now that David—Cassidy's father—is gone, I needed to think about earning a living."

"What about modeling?" I ask her.

"Been there, done that," she replies. "Crazy hours, too much travel. Anyway, I pitched this idea to the Food Network a few months ago, and I just got word from a producer there, Fred Goldberg, that it's a go."

"Did you say *Fred*?" says Cassidy.

Her mother nods. "Why?"

"No reason." Cassidy looks over at me and grins. I grin back. She starts to bounce up and down.

Her mother gives a tentative bounce. "Hey, this is fun," she says, and in a flash I'm bouncing too, and then Emma and Jess and their mothers and my mother jump onto the beds and we're all bouncing. Emma grabs a pillow and swats her mother with it. Her mother grabs one and swats back. Soon, we're all leaping from one bed to the other, smacking each other with pillows and laughing hysterically.

"Did you know that the Alcotts used to have pillow fights every Saturday night?" says Mrs. Hawthorne breathlessly. "Bronson thought it was good for the children."

"I think it's good for adults, too," Mrs. Delaney replies. "I haven't laughed this hard in ages."

Emma swats Mrs. Sloane. "That is just so cool!" she cries. "Your own TV show!"

Heather Vogel Frederick

"And you'll love New York," says my mother.

Cassidy suddenly stops jumping. "Wait a minute," she says. "Does this mean we have to move to New York?"

The bouncing stops. We all hug our pillows. Cassidy's mother kneels down beside her and puts her hands on her shoulders. "No, honey," she replies. "That's the best part. I told Fred that no way was I uprooting you and Courtney again so soon. I'll have to fly down a couple of times a month for meetings, but I agreed to do the show on one condition: that we film it at home in our kitchen in Concord."

Out of the corner of my eye I see Jess look over at her mother. Her expression is sad.

Mrs. Hawthorne catapults off the bed and crosses to the table. She picks up the phone. "Room service?" she says. "We need eight hot fudge sundaes up here in room 212 on the double."

"Phoebe, it's nearly midnight!" says my mother, shocked. "What are you thinking?"

"I'm thinking we need to celebrate all this good news," Emma's mother replies gleefully. "First Megan, then Cassidy, and now this. Who can sleep?"

We all scatter to change into our pajamas, and a few minutes later a trolley arrives bearing our sundaes.

"To good news," says Mrs. Hawthorne, raising her spoon in salute.

"To good friends," says my mother.

"And most of all, to the Mother-Daughter Book Club!" says Mrs. Sloane, and we all dig in.

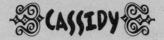

CASSIDY

"'When will he come home, Marmee?' asked Beth, with a little quiver in her voice."

"This is your daughter?"

We're standing backstage on the set of *HeartBeats*, and I'm wearing my lucky Red Sox T-shirt, the one I had on last night at the game. In the pocket of my shorts is my autographed baseball. I keep pulling it out and looking at it. I still can't believe it's mine.

The soap opera's head stylist is looking at me like you might look at something you discovered stuck to the bottom of your shoe. She glances over at my mother and then back at me again. Bored, I gnaw on a hangnail. We get this reaction all the time. Nobody can believe we're related.

I let out a little burp. My mother sighs. Our trip to my mom's new TV studio was really fun. The breakfast was amazing—no big surprise there. It *is* the Food Network, after all, not ESPN. We all stuffed our faces. Mom introduced us to Fred, her new producer, and we helped him and his staff brainstorm ideas for the show. Mrs. Hawthorne suggested featuring a Mother-Daughter Book Club tea sometime, and Fred went nuts for it. He wants us all to be on that episode. I don't know if I really want to be on TV, but I guess it will be okay. Emma says Becca Chadwick and the Fab Three will die when they find out. I figure that alone is a good enough reason to do it.

Turns out Mrs. Wong and Mrs. Hawthorne had so many good ideas that Fred asked them to be consultants for the show. Mrs. Wong, because she knows everything about organic and natural foods and my mother wants the show to feature healthy cooking, and Mrs. Hawthorne because she's a librarian and knows just about everything else under the sun. And whatever she doesn't know, she can find the answers to.

The stylist is still staring at me. Beside me, Queen Clementine draws herself up. She puts her arm around me. "Yes, Cassidy Ann is my daughter," she replies briskly. "Isn't she a beauty?"

I stare up at her, astonished. I can't ever remember Mom calling me a beauty. She's always too busy trying to fix my hair, and wipe the dirt off my face, and get me not to slouch.

"Cassidy plays hockey," my mother continues. "She was MVP—most valuable player—for the Concord Comets last season. Perhaps you've heard of them? They won the New England regional championship for the PeeWee division last season."

"Really?" says the stylist, pursing her lips. "Charming."

She doesn't sound charmed. She plucks at my T-shirt—which really doesn't smell all that bad—with her thumb and forefinger and leads me over to a salon chair. An assistant appears. "We have our work cut out for us with this one," the head stylist murmurs. She cocks her head and eyes me critically in the mirror. "Hmmm. Let's see—good bone structure, nice eyes, freckles aren't too awful, but the hair—" She pauses and shudders. "Beyond belief." She snaps her fingers and her assistant jumps. "Shampoo, and plenty of detangler."

I am led off to a sink in the corner of the studio's makeup department. When I return, dripping, all the salon chairs are occupied. The entire Mother-Daughter Book Club is busy being fussed over by *HeartBeat's* staff of stylists.

After everyone's finished being primped, we change into the outfits we shopped for yesterday. Mrs. Wong is the biggest surprise. My mother picked out these slim black pants for her, and high-heeled sandals— Mrs. Wong in high heels! Amazing!—and she's wearing this short-sleeved red silk dragon lady-style tunic, the kind with the little buttons down the front that look like knots. It's pretty cool-looking. I might even think about wearing something like that. Plus, the hair stylist did something to her hair that makes it look softer, and she's got makeup on, to boot.

"Lily, you are a vision!" says my mother, and Mrs. Wong looks embarrassed but pleased.

Mrs. Hawthorne and Emma are wearing matching dresses, which sounds incredibly dorky but somehow isn't, and Jess's hair has been twisted up into what Megan informs me is a french braid. Mrs. Delaney tucks a blue flower into it that's the same shade as her sundress. She gives her a hug. "You look beautiful, sweetie," she says.

Mrs. Delaney is slathered with way too much makeup, but that's the way they do it on soap operas, I guess. She's wearing this green ballgown thing for the day's shoot, which is about to start. She told us at breakfast that we're going to watch them film a very dramatic scene where Judd Chance decides to leave Larissa LaRue after a fancy charity event.

"Now you look more like Clementine's daughter," the head stylist says, looking at me approvingly.

I stare at myself in the mirror and scratch at my dress. It's a little itchy, but it's cool at least. It's hot under all these lights in here. Looking at myself feels weird, like looking at someone else. My hair is all smooth and shiny, and they cut it shorter so that it slants forward a bit, just below my chin. Whenever I turn my head, it swings a little, which is distracting. I keep reaching up to shove it behind my ears, and my mother keeps grabbing my hand. "Leave it alone," she says. "It looks great."

A man with a clipboard comes striding in, along with the actor who plays Judd. Megan suddenly goes all red in the face. I watch with interest as she sneaks little glances at him. Maybe Zach Norton is on the way out.

"I'm not at all happy with this dialogue," the man with the clipboard says to Mrs. Delaney. She and Judd Chance peer over his shoulder as he taps the script with his pencil. "This line here, after Judd tells Larissa that he's leaving for California, and you say, 'Oh, my darling, I only wish you'd reconsider!' It just doesn't ring true."

"That's because it's too nice," Emma pipes up. "Larissa LaRue would never say that. She has more backbone. She's put up with way too much from Judd already. She should say something smart-alecky like, 'Can I help you pack?'"

The man with the clipboard looks over at her in surprise. "And who are you?"

"That's my daughter Jess's friend Emma Hawthorne," says Mrs. Delaney.

The director looks down at the script. He frowns. "You know, that's exactly right," he says. "Perfect, in fact." He looks up. "How do you spell your last name?"

Emma tells him, and he makes a note.

"Well, young lady, I'm going to see to it that you are added to the credits for this episode as an assistant writer," he says, winking at Mrs. Delaney.

Emma's mouth pops open. I slap her a high five. "Way to go, Hawthorne!"

Her mother beams. "That's my girl," she says proudly.

"It looks like Megan's career isn't the only one that's been launched this trip," says Mrs. Wong, as the man with the clipboard strides out, followed by Judd Chance.

"New York must be our lucky city," says Mrs. Sloane.

Only Jess doesn't have anything to say. She's been quiet all afternoon, and every time I look at her I catch her watching her mother.

We file onto the set and take our seats to watch the filming. It's kind of boring, actually—there are a zillion takes for each scene, and there's way too much kissing. But Mrs. Delaney seems really happy to have us here, and she keeps waving at Jess between takes.

The director finally calls for a break, and I head for the water fountain. As I bend over to take a sip, Jess and her mother walk by. They don't see me.

Heather Vogel Frederick

"When are you coming home?" I hear Jess ask.

"Oh, sweetie, I'm not sure," her mother replies.

"Couldn't you work out a deal like Cassidy's mom did? Couldn't they film *HeartBeats* in Concord?"

Mrs. Delaney sighs. "Jess, I really, really wish I could be both places at once. But you've got to understand—this is the chance in a lifetime for an actress my age. I'm forty, honey. I'm not just starting out. This could be the last crack I get at a real career."

"But don't you miss us?" Jess pleads, and I can tell that she's crying. I stay bent over the water fountain, not daring to move a muscle.

"Of course I miss you!" her mother says. "I miss you so much, I can hardly stand it sometimes!"

"Then why don't you come home?"

A loudspeaker above my head crackles to life. "All cast members back on the set!"

"Please try and understand, honey," Mrs. Delaney says.

"Understand what? That acting is more important to you than we are?" Jess's tone is bitter.

"Now, people!" barks the loudspeaker.

"I have to go," says Mrs. Delaney. "We'll talk about this more later, okay?"

She hurries back toward the set. Jess slumps onto a low stool nearby and buries her head in her arms.

I straighten up and watch her for a minute. Then I tiptoe over. "Um, Jess," I whisper.

She doesn't reply.

I sit down on the floor beside her. "I couldn't help overhearing," I tell her. I pat her awkwardly on the back. "Jess, I'm really sorry."

Jess looks up. "I wish—I wish—" She shakes her head miserably. "I just wish everything could be the way it was before."

"I know," I reply, thinking of my father. "Me, too." I pass her a tissue and she blows her nose. Then I help her to her feet and we go back to our seats.

Later, in the dark theater on Broadway, as we watch Marmee and Jo and the March sisters go through their trials and tribulations, I think about everything that's happened these last couple of days. My hand slips into the pocket of my dress, where I've stashed my souvenir baseball. Zach Norton is going to be green with envy when he sees it. All of us got a little piece of our heart's desire this trip, I think to myself. All except Jess. She's the only one returning home to Concord empty-handed, leaving what she most wants behind.

I watch the play some more, and I get a little lump in my throat thinking about the sad part that's coming soon when Beth dies. Mom was right, I did cry when we read that part of the story together. I couldn't help it. It reminded me so much of Dad.

I look over at Jess. At least I know that the accident wasn't something he chose to have happen. I can't imagine what it must be like for Jess, knowing that her mother is choosing to live here in New York, instead of at home in Concord on Half Moon Farm. That would be hard. Really hard.

Life is so unfair sometimes.

Heather Vogel Frederick

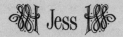 Jess

"Now and then, in this workaday world, things do happen in the delightful storybook fashion, and what a comfort it is."

"Jess!" my father hollers up the stairs. "Will you see if you can round up your brothers? We're going to be late! Oh, and make sure the chickens are in their pen too, while you're at it."

"Chickens, brothers—it's always something," I grumble, clacking down to the kitchen in my new sandals. "Never a minute to myself."

There's no sign of Dylan and Ryan in the house, so I head for the barn to look for them, stopping by the feed bins to grab a double handful of cracked corn to lure the hens.

"Come on, girls!" I call, making encouraging clucking noises at the flock scattered around our back yard. "Come and get it!"

The chickens cock their heads when they hear me calling and make a beeline for the enticing trail I've strewn at my feet.

"Good girl, Wynonna," I say to the plump Rhode Island Red who reaches me first. "Oops, don't trample Minnie Pearl!"

Nashville's finest follows the trail I sprinkle behind me, right into the wire mesh enclosure of their pen. I fill up their water and check the feed level in the dispenser. My brothers gathered eggs this morning—that's one of their chores—but I scout the nest boxes anyway, just to be sure. In this heat, it's not good to leave fresh eggs outside for too long.

I find my brothers parachuting from the hayloft with Mom's best linen tablecloth and drag them protesting back to the house, where I throw the tablecloth in the laundry hamper and clean the twins off as best I can. Sometimes I wish I could just throw them in the hamper too.

"Why do we have to dress up?" whines Dylan.

"Because it's a party," I reply calmly, brushing his hay-strewn hair.

"I hate parties," says Ryan.

"You do not," I tell him. "Remember your birthday? And how about Christmas at the Sloanes?"

He brightens. "Will there be another sleigh ride?"

"No, silly, it's August."

"How about presents?" asks Dylan, trying to squirm out of my grasp.

I grip him more firmly. "I don't know. Maybe. If you're really good."

Both boys perk up at this news.

I open the fridge and take out a big plastic container. Lifting the cover, I show my brothers the rows of cupcakes. "There'll be treats at the party too," I tell them, and they follow me out to the truck as docilely as the chickens followed the trail of corn to their pen.

Sugar is waiting patiently by the passenger door.

"You can't come, Sugar," I tell her. "You need to stay here and keep an eye on the farm."

Heather Vogel Frederick

With a deep sigh of resignation, she slinks over to the maple tree and flops down in the shade. She drops her head on her paws and gazes at me reproachfully.

My dad comes out of the barn, whistling. "Everybody ready?" he says. He smiles at me. "You look nice."

"Thanks." I'm wearing the blue sundress that Mom and Mrs. Sloane helped me pick out in New York for the theater.

We all climb into the truck. I hear a thud in the back and whirl around. I frown at my brothers. "You boys knock that off! You need to be on your best behavior today at the Hawthornes'."

"Knock what off?" they reply, their eyes wide with innocence.

"Whatever it is that you're doing back there."

"Whew, it's a scorcher," says Dad, flipping on the air-conditioning.

We head into town toward the Hawthornes', who are hosting an end-of-summer celebration for the Mother-Daughter Book Club. We pass Sleepy Hollow, but when we get to Monument Square, instead of turning right toward Emma's, we turn left.

"Where are you going?" I ask. "Lowell Road is the other way."

"You'll see," my father says mysteriously.

We drive along for a mile or so, and then he pulls into the parking lot in front of a big brown house.

"Orchard House? Why are we stopping here?" I ask. "It's closed on Sundays."

"Is that right?" my father replies, smiling. He's very cheerful today.

He gets out of the truck. I open my door and climb out too. As I do so, Emma and her family pull in beside us.

"Surprise!" says Mrs. Hawthorne, leaning out the window. "Welcome to the Mother-Daughter Book Club picnic!"

"We're having it here?" I say. "At Louisa May Alcott's house?"

Mrs. Hawthorne nods, beaming. "I got special permission. I have a friend who's on the board of trustees."

My father goes around to the back of the pickup. "I've got the folding table right here, Nick," he says to Mr. Hawthorne, unlatching the tailgate. He jumps back, startled, as Sugar's head pops up. She looks at us happily, panting.

"Sugar!" I cry. "You little stowaway!"

"What are we going to do with you?" Dad scolds. "I can't leave you out here in the truck in this heat."

"I'm sure it's fine if she joins us, as long as we keep her outside," says Mrs. Hawthorne.

The Wongs' hybrid sedan pulls in, along with the Sloanes' minivan. It's just Cassidy and her mother because Courtney is at cheerleading camp this week. We carry everything for the picnic around to the back of the house.

"Let's set up in the shade," says Mrs. Sloane. "It's so hot out."

As the dads and Darcy busy themselves setting up the long folding table and chairs, my little brothers buzz excitedly around the food.

"Will there be presents?" asks Ryan again hopefully.

Mrs. Hawthorne smiles at him. "A very special one, just for you," she tells him. "I promise."

Before I can get her to tell me what it is, Mrs. Sloane calls me over

Heather Vogel Frederick

to help her with the table. Cassidy and Emma and Megan and I spread out the tablecloth and set out paper plates and napkins and plastic silverware.

"Put this in the middle, would you, Jess?" Mrs. Sloane says, handing me a big mason jar with a bouquet of daisies in it.

"We'll keep the food covered until after the tour," says Mrs. Wong. "Well, all except for this little corner." She lifts up a piece of foil and sneaks out two deviled eggs, which she passes to my brothers. "That'll help tide you over, boys."

The back door of Orchard House opens and Mrs. Hawthorne's friend appears. "I'm ready any time you are," she says.

"You gentlemen are welcome to join us," says Mrs. Hawthorne, but Darcy and our dads have settled into the lawn chairs in the shade, and my brothers are happily running around chasing Sugar.

"I think we'll wait out here," says my father. He lifts a plastic cup of lemonade in salute. "You ladies go enjoy yourselves."

I've been through Orchard House a zillion times before—with my mother, with my school, with my Brownie troop, plus Emma and I ride our bikes over almost every summer—but somehow it's different this time.

We walk through the house with Mrs. Hawthorne's friend, and it feels more alive to me now. Louisa's mood pillow, the dining room where the Alcott sisters put on their plays, May's artwork and Beth's piano—it's like they were all just here, and stepped outside for a walk or something.

Upstairs in Louisa's bedroom, we all grow quiet. Even Cassidy. Emma takes her mother's hand.

"This is the desk where Miss Alcott wrote *Little Women*," says our tour guide, pointing to a semicircular wooden table built between the two front windows. "Louisa's father made it for her. It was unusual at the time because it wasn't considered proper for women to have desks of their own."

Emma reaches out and touches it with her finger. I wonder if she's thinking of her own desk at home. Over the mantel is a painting of an owl that Louisa's sister May drew for her. I examine it closely. It's beautiful, and accurate, too. "May must have been a naturalist just like you, Jess," says Mrs. Hawthorne.

Megan goes over to the bed, and examines the silk dress spread across it.

"That's Anna's wedding dress," our guide tells her.

"Her real one?" asks Megan, eyes wide.

Mrs. Hawthorne's friend nods. "Yes, the very one that Louisa used as the model for Meg's in the story. We usually only put it out during May, which is wedding month at Orchard House, but I thought you girls might enjoy seeing it so I got it out of storage. Anna made it herself."

Megan tugs on her mother's sleeve. "Look at these tiny stitches, Mom!" she says. "Aren't they beautiful?"

"And so even," agrees her mother. "It's amazing, considering she didn't have a sewing machine."

Heather Vogel Frederick

Looking at all the other girls, I can't help it. Tears well up in my eyes. It's so unfair that my mother isn't here today! She would have loved seeing all this, especially the props for the plays, like Roderigo's boots—the real ones that Louisa made. But she's not, and I blink back my tears and remind myself sternly that my life is not a storybook. Not every tale has a happy ending. That's just the way it is. People die, like Cassidy's father did, and people leave us, like my mother did. It happened to the Alcotts, and to *Little Women*'s March family, too.

We tour May's room, with the paintings and sketches on the walls. "The Alcotts encouraged all their daughters to develop their talents," explains our guide, and the mothers exchange glances and smile.

Back downstairs, our tour comes to an end in the living room. I look around. The house looks bigger on the outside than it is. It's actually quite cozy inside, like the Hawthornes' little Cape Cod–style house. And simple, like Half Moon Farm. And pretty, like the Sloanes' Victorian. And—well, it's not at all like the Wongs', except for the trees outside.

"I think I would have liked the Alcotts," I say.

Mrs. Hawthorne puts her arm around me and gives me a squeeze. "They would have *loved* you, Jess!"

Back outside, we all thank Mrs. Hawthorne's friend.

"My pleasure," she says. "I have some work to finish up here in the office, but you all have fun, and let me know if you need anything."

"Let's eat," says Cassidy.

We take our seats around the table. There are party favors on every plate, and we open them. The boys and dads all get wooden puzzles, and for us there are refrigerator magnets with quotes from Louisa May Alcott on them. Mine says "There is always light behind the clouds."

Is that true? I wonder, looking up at the sky through the trees. The sun is shining brightly and there are hardly any clouds, just some high, thin ones way off in the distance. But there seems to be an awfully big cloud hanging over my life right now.

Mr. Hawthorne stands up and raises his lemonade glass.

"A toast to the lovely ladies of the Mother-Daughter Book Club," he says. "Oh, and gentleman, too." He nods at my dad, who smiles and nods back. We all toast the book club and then we dig in. There are chicken salad sandwiches that Mr. Hawthorne made and deviled eggs and potato chips and Mrs. Sloane's homemade pickles and sliced watermelon, and for dessert, my cupcakes.

"How about a game of croquet?" asks Mrs. Hawthorne when we're finished.

As we're setting up, Emma comes over to me. "Remember in the book when Fred Vaughn cheated at 'Camp Laurence'?" she asks.

"I promise I won't," I tell her, promptly whacking her ball into the woods.

The afternoon shadows are lengthening as we head for the final wicket. It's my turn again and I line up to take my shot, but before I can do so Sugar, who is tied to a nearby tree, suddenly starts to whine.

"What is it, girl?" I ask. "What's the matter?"

Sugar's gaze is fixed on Orchard House. She looks up at me beseechingly.

Heather Vogel Frederick

"Go ahead and let her off her leash, Jess," says my father. He's smiling. All the grown-ups are smiling, in fact.

I shrug and unsnap her leash. Sugar makes a beeline for the side of the house, barking joyfully. I look over to see what's caught her attention. A squirrel, maybe? But no, it's not a squirrel. It's something bigger. Something about the size of a dog. In fact, it *is* a dog.

"Spice!" I cry in surprise. Someone is with her and I can't see who it is because the sun is in my eyes. And then all of a sudden I know who it is and I drop my mallet and I'm running, tripping over tree roots and pelting down the sloping lawn to where my mother is standing, her arms open as wide as the sky. I hurl myself into them.

"Mom!" I cry, and she pulls me to her. Her face is wet and so is mine and we're both crying, and then my little brothers are there and she flings her arms around them as well.

"It's like when Mr. March comes home from the war," I hear Megan say in wonder.

"Only better," adds Cassidy, who is beside her a little ways off with the rest of the Mother-Daughter Book Club.

Now Dad joins us and the five of us stand with our arms around one other, breathing each other in. Sugar and Spice are running in circles at our feet.

"Are you just back for the party?" I whisper, pressing my forehead into my mother's shoulder.

I don't look at her. I can hardly bear to hear her answer and at the same time I can hardly bear not to.

She lifts my chin with her finger and regards me tenderly. "No, honey," she says, shaking her head. "I'm not just back for the party."

I feel suddenly breathless. "Do you mean—"

She nods.

"But what about Larissa LaRue? What about *HeartBeats*?"

"The only thing my heart beats for now is right here in my arms," she replies, kissing my brothers and me and smiling up at my dad. "I had a talk with the show's producers. Larissa LaRue has conveniently fallen into a mysterious coma, where she'll remain for a while until we figure something more permanent out."

"Like what?" I ask.

"Something that lets me balance my love of acting with my even greater love of my family," she replies. "Guest spots, maybe. Or maybe rearranging the shooting schedule so I can split my time between New York and Concord." My mother looks at me, and her expression is serious. "I thought a lot about what you said to me in New York earlier this summer, Jess. The truth is, nothing is more important to me than you all are. There will always be stages to act on and parts to play, but there's only one Delaney family at Half Moon Farm."

Behind me, Emma sighs. "I love happy endings," she says.

So do I, I think to myself. *So do I.*

And my heart splits with joy and soars upward, high above the sun-dappled lawn, high above the rustling trees, high above Orchard House and Walden Pond and white-steepled Concord, and skimming through the clouds—*cirrus radiatus*—spreads its wings and heads for home.

Heather Vogel Frederick

"In most families there comes, now and then, a year full of events; this has been such a one, but it ends well after all."

—Little Women

Mother-Daughter Book Club Questions

Each of the four girls is very different and unique in her own way. Which character do you identify with most and why?

Louisa May Alcott's *Little Women* is a classic that has been enjoyed by millions. Have you ever read it?

If so, what is your favorite part?

If not, does this book make you want to read it?

All the mothers have their own unique personalities also. Which one reminds you most of the parent or guardian in your life?

At points, some of the girls can be pretty mean to each other. Does this reflect reality in your mind?

Are there girls or boys in your school like that?

If so, why do you think that is?

The Mother-Daughter Book Club means a lot to each of the girls and their mothers by the end of the story. Does it make you want to join a mother-daughter book club?

Do you think there is one in your area?

If not, would you start one?

If you had to compare your favorite character in the book to one of your favorite celebrities—who would it be?

What do you think is the turning point of the book?

The mothers and daughters have a lot of disagreements in the book—should Cassidy be a hockey player or a figure skater?

Should Megan be a designer or a scientist?

Should Jess's mom come home from New York City or follow her dreams?

Do you agree with the daughters or the mothers in each of these situations?

Why?

Each of the four girls have specific personality traits: Why do you think Jess is so shy?

Why do you think Emma is self-conscious?

Why do you think Megan is eager to be popular?

And why do you think Cassidy has trouble getting along her mother and a lot of her peers?

Did you believe that everything would work out well as it does in the book?

Would you change anything about the ending?

At the Christmas party, Emma receives a bookmark with a quote from Louisa May Alcott on it: "I am not afraid of storms, for I am learning how to sail my ship." Emma says, "Somehow I don't think she's talking about sailing. She's talking about life." What storms have the members of the Mother-Daughter Book Club weathered in their lives? In what ways are they learning how to "sail their ships"?

How about you—have you weathered any storms in your life?

And in what ways are you learning how to "sail your ship"?

At their book club meetings, the girls often learn "fun facts" about Louisa May Alcott. Which of these did you find most interesting?

Can you think of a few "fun facts" about Emma, Jess, Megan, and Cassidy?

And if someone were to list "fun facts" about you, what would that list include?

Author's Note

Seven of the happiest years of my childhood were spent in Concord, Massachusetts, just down the road from where Louisa May Alcott and her family once lived at Orchard House. Like Louisa, I spent hours exploring the woods and meadows behind our home and around town. Like Louisa, my sisters and I often put on plays for our family and friends. And like Louisa, reading books and writing stories were two of the main passions of my life. Every summer I would ride my bike over to Orchard House and take the tour (it cost about thirty-five cents back then!), and dream of being an author just like Louisa someday.

Fast-forward several decades. To her own astonishment, the young dreamer has indeed grown up to be an author, with books of her own on the shelf. One day her editor asks if she'd be interested in writing a story set in her old hometown, about a mother-daughter book club that's reading *Little Women*.

How could the dreamer-turned-author say anything but, "Yes, of course!"?

Then came one of those ironic quirks with which life abounds. In one more "like Louisa" coincidence, I discovered that just as my editor had asked if I'd be interested in writing this book, so a century and a half ago Louisa's editor had asked if she'd consider writing the book that eventually became *Little Women*. At that point in her career, Louisa was quite content penning her "blood and thunder" tales, as she called them—thrillers aimed at an adult audience—and wasn't so sure about writing for girls. "Never liked girls or knew many, except for my sisters," she grumbled to a friend, "but our queer plays and experiences may prove interesting, though I doubt it."

Fortunately for the world, Louisa eventually agreed to give it a try. She wrote *Little Women* in the spring and summer of 1868, seated at the half-moon desk her father had built for her between the two front windows of her bedroom at Orchard House. The book struck an instant chord with readers, and its universal themes of love, home, and happiness have continued to resonate down the years, for as Cyrus Bartol once said of Louisa, "She unlatches the door to one house and ... all find it is their house which they enter."

The Mother-Daughter Book Club is my modest homage to this talented writer and her enduring tale, my gift of thanks for the inspiration she provided me in childhood.

I also want to thank my brilliant editor, Alyssa Eisner-Henkin, not only for the spark of this story but also for entrusting me with it, and for her unflagging encouragement and enthusiasm all along the way. Thanks, too, are due to my stellar agent Barry Goldblatt for his wisdom, counsel, and care, and to my always-game-for-an-adventure sister Lisa Carper, with whom I spent a delightful day tramping about our childhood haunts. Dear friend Jonatha Wey likewise generously chauffeured me around Concord and brought me up to date on the changes in the town since I'd lived there. Helen Quigley and her family (husband Mark and children Samuel, Neil, and Lucinda) instructed me in all things hockey (any errors that remain are entirely my own);

Author's Note

Arthur Wheeler guided me through many of Concord's historic byways; Roz Ault and the wonderful staff of Orchard House provided an informative tour and patiently answered many questions; Ann Carper fortuitously shared Geraldine Brooks's sublime "March" when inspiration flagged. Last, but first and foremost in my heart, deepest thanks to my cherished husband, Steve, and our sons Ian and Ben for providing me with companionship, laughter, and love always.

Here's an excerpt from Heather Vogel Frederick's newest chapter in THE MOTHER-DAUGHTER BOOK CLUB books:

The Mother-Daughter Book Club: Chapter Two

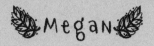

Megan

"Well, this is a pretty kettle of fish."
—*Anne of Green Gables*

"What are you girls up to out there?"

I swear all mothers have radar that doesn't quit.

"Nothing, Mom!" Jess calls back, motioning frantically to Emma and me.

Giggling, the two of us scoop up the evidence—garlic powder, cinnamon, peppermint extract, and blue food coloring—and hastily stuff it back into the spice cupboard.

"Doesn't sound like nothing to me." We hear Mrs. Delaney's chair scrape on the dining room floor as she pushes back from the table and comes in to the kitchen to investigate.

Emma and I quickly wipe the grins off our faces. Jess leans back casually against the counter, blocking our concoction from view.

"Hmmm," says Mrs. Delaney, scanning the kitchen suspiciously.

She spots the open spice cupboard and lifts an eyebrow.

"Uh, we were thinking of baking cookies," Jess explains, which isn't technically a lie even though we decided not to because the kitchen is sweltering.

Normally, any of our mothers would see through this in a flash, but Mrs. Delaney seems kind of distracted today. She shakes her head and sighs. "Please don't bake anything, girls. It's hot enough in here already without turning the oven on. We've got peppermint ice cream—you can have some of that if you want a snack." She opens the freezer door and sticks her head inside. "A day like today kind of makes you wish it was winter, doesn't it?"

"Or that we had air-conditioning," says Jess mournfully.

Mrs. Delaney pulls her head out again and gives her a regretful smile. "Maybe someday, honey. Right now we have other priorities." She looks over at Emma. The smile disappears. "Emma Hawthorne, you must be roasting in that turtleneck! Didn't you offer her a T-shirt, Jess?"

Jess looks uncomfortable. "Uh—"

"I forgot to bring something to change into after school, and nothing of Jess's fits me, Mrs. Delaney," Emma replies matter-of-factly, patting her stomach. Emma is a little on the plump side and Jess is really petite.

"Well for Pete's sake, you should have said something," Mrs. Delaney tells her. "We have plenty of things around here that will work for you. Hang on a sec."

She trots upstairs. I glance over at Emma. Emma is one of my best friends, but she's not exactly the fashion queen of Concord, Massachusetts. I mean, I like to dress up for the first day of school, too, but a turtleneck on a day like this? You'd think she'd know by now that the beginning of September is pretty much still summer everywhere, except maybe Alaska. At least she picked a good color. Purple goes well with her brown eyes and curly brown hair.

Mrs. Delaney reappears and tosses Emma a white T-shirt with a *HeartBeats* logo on it. "Try this," she says.

HeartBeats is the soap opera that Mrs. Delaney was on last year. You'd never guess by looking at her now that she's an actress. When we visited her in New York this past summer, she was all glamorous. Now—well, now she looks the way she always did. Today, for instance, she's wearing jeans and a faded Red Sox T-shirt. She's still pretty and everything—really pretty, just like Jess, with the same sparkly blue eyes, though Mrs. Delaney's hair is dark, not blond like Jess's—but she looks ordinary too. Like a mom. I wonder if she misses all the makeup and clothes and stuff from her acting job. I sure would. But Mrs. Delaney seems really happy to be back home at Half Moon Farm.

"How's your mom doing, Megan?" she asks me. "We missed her yesterday at yoga class."

"She just got elected to the board of the Concord Riverkeepers," I tell her. "Yesterday was their first meeting." My mother's kind of a nature freak. If something on the planet needs saving or protecting, you can bet Lily Wong is there on the front lines.

"Oh, that's right, she told us about that," Mrs. Delaney replies. "I guess I forgot." She spots the pile of mail on the counter where Jess left it. "Bills, bills, nothing but bills," she grumbles, flipping through the envelopes. Shaking her head, she disappears back into the dining room.

As soon as her mother is out of sight, Jess grabs the jar of blue liquid from the counter behind her and sticks it in her T-shirt pocket. Then she gets three bowls from the cupboard and dishes up some ice cream for each of us. Crossing the kitchen, she beckons us to follow. One of her chickens—Johnny Cash or Elvis or something, I can't keep their names straight—darts in the minute she opens the screen door. Jess nabs it and it lets out a big squawk.

"You know the rules, Loretta," Jess tells it firmly. "No chickens in the house!"

Sometimes I still can't believe I'm friends with somebody who talks to chickens. Or somebody who even has chickens.

Emma and I follow Jess to the barn. Mr. Delaney let us fix up an old storage room in the hayloft for a secret hangout. Not that it's much of a secret, what with Jess's little brothers always sneaking around.

Right now, though, there's no sign of them. We scared them off after we caught them spying on us in Jess's room when we were changing out of our school clothes. They'll turn up eventually, though—they always turn up—and when they do, we'll be ready for them thanks to our concoction, which is now safely in Jess's pocket.

"I wish it could stay summer forever," sighs Emma, climbing up the hayloft ladder behind me.

"Me too," echoes Jess.

Not me, I think, but I don't say anything. I've always liked the first day of school. Mostly because I get to wear one of the new outfits that I spend all summer picking out. I can't help it—I like clothes. I want to be a fashion designer when I grow up.

"Hey, did you guys see Zach Norton at assembly this morning?" I ask them. "He's so tall! He must have grown about a foot over the summer." I take a bite of ice cream and give Emma a sidelong glance. "He's cuter than ever, too."

Emma shrugs, but her cheeks turn as pink as her ice cream. Lately she's been telling us that she doesn't have a crush on Zach anymore. Jess and Cassidy and I are pretty sure she still does, though. Not that I'd mind if she didn't—the way I see it, the fewer girls lined up hoping Zach Norton will notice them, the better my chances are.

The fact that we both like Zach is one of the only things Emma and I have in common, when you come right down to it. We look different, for starters. I'm Asian American—she's not. She's a bookworm—I'm not. I love fashion and clothes—she could care less. And although she's not off-the-charts smart like Jess, she's a good student. Me, I just scrape by, which drives my parents nuts. Somehow, despite our differences, we're still good friends.

Emma sticks out her lower lip and puffs at her bangs, which are sticking to her forehead. It's even hotter out here in the barn than it was in the Delaney's kitchen. Jess turns on a table fan and aims it straight at the old sofa where the three of us are sitting.

"Can you believe we're in seventh grade now?" she says. "Just think —two more years and we'll be in high school."

We eat our ice cream for a while as we think this over.

"We're going to be teenagers this year," Emma adds. "We're practically grown-ups!"

Sometimes I feel like I've been looking forward to being a teenager forever. I can't wait until I'm old enough to drive. And have a summer job. And I especially can't wait until I'm old enough to date.

"So do either of you have any classes with Zach this year?" I ask, trying to sound casual.

"Zach! Zach! Ooooo, Zach Norton!" squeal a pair of voices behind us.

We whirl around to see Dylan and Ryan, Jess's twin brothers, emerge from under a pile of old horse blankets in the corner.

"I TOLD YOU TO QUIT SPYING ON US!" hollers Jess.

She launches off the sofa toward them, but they're too fast for her. Shrieking in alarm, they duck past Jess on the way out the door. The three of us are close on their heels. The boys fling themselves over the edge of the loft and tumble into the pile of hay below. Jess dives after them. So does Emma. I hesitate. My friends all love doing this, but it always seems like a long way down to me.

I close my eyes and force myself to jump.

"Ouch!" I cry when I land, wishing I were still wearing my good school jeans and not my shorts. The hay is stiff and prickly, and it jabs into my bare legs. I scramble off of it as quickly as I can and run after Emma and Jess.

We corner her brothers by the chicken coop.

"Pest Control 101," Jess whispers to Emma and me, taking the small jar from her T-shirt pocket. "Watch and learn." She holds it up. The blue liquid inside shimmers in the September sunlight. "Gee," she says, "too bad my brothers are such little weasels—I was going to share some of this with them."

"What is it?" one of them asks cautiously. Like the chickens, I can't tell Dylan and Ryan apart.

Jess glances around, like maybe somebody is listening, and her voice drops to a whisper. "It's an invisibility potion."

Her brothers' eyes widen.

"Really?" says one of them.

Jess nods. "If you drink it, you'll disappear just like that." She snaps her fingers and looks over at Emma and me. "Isn't that right?"

Emma nods. "Yup. You'll vanish right into thin air."

"Vaporize," I tell them.

"Dematerialize," adds Jess for good measure.

The three of us are smothering grins. Emma's family invented this thing called the synonym game. I used to think it was dumb—actually, I still do—but it's kind of addictive.

"Please can't we try it?" one of the twins begs.

"C'mon, Jess!" says the other.

Jess shakes her head. "No way. You broke your promise. You said you wouldn't spy on us anymore."

The boys exchange a glance. With their blond curls and brown, puppy-dog eyes, they look like angels, but there's hardly anything angelic about them. "Double trouble," Jess calls them. "Pests with a capital P," and she's right. I still think they're kind of cute, though. I wish I had a brother or sister, but my parents decided on just one child. Me. My mother tried to explain it to me once—something about zero population growth. Another one of her schemes to save the world, as usual.

"We're sorry, Jess. Right, Dylan?"

"Yeah, really sorry," says Dylan. "We promise never to do it again."

"Cross your hearts and hope to die?" Jess demands.

They both nod.

"Well, I guess in that case . . ." Slowly, tantalizingly, she unscrews the lid and passes the jar to Dylan.

He sniffs it cautiously. "Pew!" he cries, and hands it to his brother. "You first."

Ryan takes a sip and makes a face.

"You have to drink more than that or it won't work," Jess tells him.

Grimacing, her brother gulps down half the liquid, and then passes the jar to his brother, coughing.

"Yuck! That is gross!" Dylan sputters after he finishes off the rest.

I have to bite my lip to keep from laughing. Beside me, Emma is doing the same. The twins crowd around us. "Is it working?" they demand.

We pretend to examine them.

"You're fading at the edges," Emma says.

"It probably takes a minute or two," I explain.

Suddenly, Jess jumps back, her eyes wide in mock disbelief. "Wow, guys, look! It worked! They're gone!"

Emma shades her eyes with her hand and scans the backyard. "Where are they? Where did Dylan and Ryan go? Do you see them anywhere, Megan?"

I shake my head, still trying not to burst out laughing. Was I this gullible when I was seven?

Dancing around us, Dylan and Ryan chant, "Nyah, nyah! We're invisible!"

They stop and stare at each other.

"Hey, how come I can see Ryan?" says Dylan.

"Yeah, and how come I can see Dylan?" says Ryan.

"It's because you're both invisible," Jess explains, making it sound perfectly logical. "Invisible people can always see each other. It's the people who aren't invisible who can't see you."

Just then there's a crunch of gravel behind us. We turn around to see Cassidy Sloane flying up the driveway on her bike. She skids to a stop right in front of the twins.

"Hi guys," she says to them.

Dylan's eyes narrow. "How come Cassidy can see us? She's not invisible."

"Uh, it's because she has special powers," Jess replies. "Right, Cassidy?"

"I guess so," mutters Cassidy, not really paying attention. She must have ridden over straight from baseball, because she's still wearing her practice jersey. It's the same one she had on at school today. No back-to-school outfits for Cassidy Sloane. She cares even less about fashion than Emma does. Cassidy is a jock and proud of the fact that she's the only girl at Walden Middle School good enough to make the boys' baseball team. I notice that her face is streaked with dirt and sweat.

"You tricked us!" shrieks Ryan. "I'm going to tell mom!"

He and his brother head for the house, howling for Mrs. Delaney. A minute later Jess's mother sticks her head out the dining room window. "Jessica Delaney! You are too old to be teasing your brothers!"

"But they've been spying on us again!" Jess protests.

"I don't care what they've been doing! You quit it this instant, do you hear?"

"Yes, mom," Jess calls back.

Beside me, Emma is staring at Cassidy. "Are you okay?"

Cassidy wipes her nose on the sleeve of her jersey. I look at her face more closely. What I thought were streaks of sweat in the dirt are actually tears. I stare at her, dumbfounded. Cassidy Sloane is crying.

"Emergency session of the Mother-Daughter Book Club," Emma announces crisply. "Well, the daughter half." She tugs Cassidy toward the barn.

"Hurry, before my brothers spot us," Jess urges.

We pick up our pace to a trot. Once safely inside and out of sight, Jess leads the way back up into the hayloft, then pulls the ladder up behind us so the boys can't follow this time.

"What's going on?" Emma asks, as Cassidy flings herself face first into the pile of blankets.

"Nothing." Cassidy's voice is muffled.

"Doesn't sound like nothing," says Emma.

She and Jess sit down beside her. Jess reaches out and pats Cassidy on the back, the way I've seen her do with Sugar and Spice, the Delaney's Shetland sheepdogs. "C'mon, Cassidy," she coaxes. "You can tell us."

I sit down too. The blankets smell good. In fact, the whole barn smells good—like hay and horses and leather and old wood and other stuff all mixed together. *Eau de Barn*. I make a mental note to jot it down in my sketchbook later. It might make an interesting men's cologne.

"It's my mom," Cassidy says finally in a low voice.

Emma and Jess and I exchange a worried glance. Cassidy's dad died a couple of years ago. What if something's wrong with her mother?

"Is she okay?" asks Emma gently. "She's not sick or anything, is she?"

Cassidy sits up. "No, it's not that," she says. She draws her legs in close to her chest and rests her chin on her knees. "She's not sick," she repeats, plucking at the blankets. "It's just that she . . . she . . ." Her sentence trails off.

"She what?" I prod.

Cassidy looks up and tears start to spill from her eyes again. She swipes at them angrily. "My mother's started dating again."

About the Author

When Heather Vogel Frederick was in the sixth grade, she used to ride her bike past Louisa May Alcott's house in Concord, Massachusetts, and dream of being a writer. Today, the award-winning author of the Patience Goodspeed books and the Spy Mice series lives in Portland, Oregon, with her husband, their two teenage sons, the family's beloved Shetland sheepdog, and three fun-loving chickens.